LINGERING SOUL OF THE HOUSE

VIVIAN WARD CRUMP

Lingering Soul of the House:

This book is manufactured in the United States.

ISBN-13: 978-0-9965445-0-4
ISBN-10: 099654450X

Library of Congress   20159903798

FIRST EDITION paperback

Publisher:

M & K Literary Publishing
PO Box 6282
Louisville, KY 40206

Vivian Ward Crump

Lingering Soul of the House,

A Novel

DEDICATION

TO FAMILY AND FRIENDS
AND
MY HOME TOWN OF SALYERSVILLE, KENTUCKY

ACKNOWLEDGMENTS

God has put extraordinary family and friends in my life. For this I am thankful. Thanks to all those that have encouraged and supported me during the writing of this novel.

Lingering Soul of the House

Prologue

Six Years Earlier

The two girls ran without stopping, trying to catch the boy as he sprinted ahead of them. "Wait, Barry!" Deb squealed. Barry didn't slow down as he made it to the front door of their grandparents' farmhouse. The screen door slammed behind him.

Deb and Cassie cleared the door seconds later, making sure it didn't slam behind them. Grandma Lizzy wouldn't be happy with the noise. They made their way to the bathroom and found Barry leaning against the washbasin with a soapy cloth, scrubbing his arms and legs.

They pushed Barry to the side of the sink, wet their clothes and grabbed the only bar of Dial soap.

"Man, my arms and legs sting." Barry complained as he inspected his limbs. "I've got red stripes all over my body." His attention moved to his sister. He pulled her arm close to him in order to examine her skin. "Deb, you have them too." Barry yelped. "Does your skin hurt like mine?"

Deb pulled her arm back and focused her eyes on the rash that streaked across her limbs. Recognition flickered across her face.

"Oh, what have we done?" She blew air from her mouth onto her arms. Between puffs she asked, "Do you think the corn did it?" The three of them had been out all morning playing in one of Granddad Sam's cornfields. Deb assumed the corn must have caused the rash. "Cassie, what does your skin look like? Are you hurting too?"

Before Cassie could respond, they heard a moan from somewhere inside the house. Cassie tilted her head in the direction of the sound. Again the moaning cry pierced the air. Cassie whispered, "Was that Grandma Lizzy? Something bad must have happened. She would never cry like that. We have to find her. Maybe we can help."

The three nine year olds stood silent and motionless, listening. The sad mournful cry echoed through the house. It was a woman or maybe women. Their aching skin forgotten, the three children followed the sound of the cries. Listening to the eerie cries made their hair stand on end. Barry, trying to be brave, walked ahead of his twin sister and his cousin.

As they moved closer to the crying sound, it became more forlorn. Cassie looked at her cousin Deb and saw tears shining in her eyes ready to spill. She swallowed, trying to keep her mind from thinking about what could make her grandma cry so mournfully.

The cries led them past the living room and through the back of the house to the guest bedroom. When they got to the doorway, Barry stopped abruptly causing Deb to bump into his back. The crying stopped. As the girls peeked around Barry's back, they were shocked at what they saw. Sitting on Grandma Lizzy's ottoman in front of the vanity, with her straight, narrow back to them, sat a lady dressed in a long-sleeved, black dress that covered her whole body. The three held their breath. It seemed like hours but only seconds passed when without warning, in a smooth, fluid movement the lady in black stood and turned to face them. Her pale grey face was void of emotion. She stared past them without focusing on anything.

The room was silent. After a few seconds, Barry got his voice and his courage back. "S-s-s-orry, we thought our grandma was in here crying and we came to help her. Are you okay?" The girls inched close behind Barry.

The lady looked at the three children without moving. She stared at their faces. Cassie felt she was looking through them, almost as if she didn't see them at all. She fought the urge to run. The lady was oddly scary. Cassie stole a quick look at Deb. She was scared too. She looked back at the woman—she hadn't moved.

The longer they stood in the doorway the more uncomfortable they became. Cassie decided that Grandma Lizzy would want them to comfort her friend, so she asked, "Do you want us to go get Grandma Lizzy?" Still, the lady didn't move. She didn't cry. She was completely still.

The children slowly backed out of the room and raced to see who could get out of the house first. The three squeezed through the door together. Once out of the house, they began calling for their great-grandparents. Barry motioned with his hand for the girls to stop and listen. They heard Granddad Sam calling from the vegetable garden and took off toward his voice as fast as their legs would take them. They found both of their great-grandparents leaning on their hoes in the green bean patch.

"Grandma Lizzy, the lady in the house is crying. We told her we would get you to help." Deb blurted out between deep rapid breaths.

A frown creased Grandma's mouth as she looked at Granddad. She searched each child's face. Cassie thought it odd that Grandma Lizzy was in the hot sun, yet her face was as white as a sheet and her voice cracked when she spoke to them. "There's someone in the house?"

The three children nodded in unison. Cassie volunteered, "When we asked her if she was your friend, she didn't say a word."

Granddad moved closer and asked, "What did this lady look like guys?"

"She looked sad. She had on a black dress with black lace around her neck. It looked old, like the dresses in old movies. You know, like in the westerns you watch all of the time." Cassie frowned and finished, "Her cry sounded so sad."

Barry looked at Granddad, "I could have sworn there was more than one woman crying, Granddad. We thought for sure that Grandma Lizzy was hurt. And when we went to find her we found that woman instead." Barry shook his head frowning, "Something really, really bad must have happened to that lady because she sounded so sad. And, she didn't even speak to us the whole time we were with her."

Granddad nodded. "Don't you children fret about that lady. Grandma and I know this old gal, and we'll take care of her. Now, I want you three to go play over at the barn. Grandma and I will go comfort the lady." Granddad put his hand on Grandma Lizzy's shoulder.

Cassie thought that her grandparents were spooked, but they wanted to hide it. She could tell they were scared from the way Granddad was dancing around with his answers about the lady. And, not once had Grandma Lizzy said why this lady was in her guest bedroom. Her great-grandparents hadn't told them if she was a friend or not. She got a feeling that she would be better off not knowing, so she didn't push the questions. She wanted answers, but instead followed her cousins to the barn.

That was the last time the lady was mentioned, that day or for that matter, for the remaining days of their visit. No one asked about her because they all felt that their great-grandparents didn't want to talk about it and none of them wanted to be afraid again.

One

"NOOOOOO!" Cassie felt the word erupt from deep within her. She attempted to slow her pacing although trying to look normal and reasonable was next to impossible. The last thing she wanted to do was to give her mother ammunition to use against her. Leigh had repeatedly used the argument that Cassie wasn't being reasonable. Well, of course, she wasn't. How could anyone in her predicament be "reasonable?"

She felt as if she was living in a nightmare. Taking a deep breath, she willed herself to stay calm before joining her mother for one last attempt to persuade her to change her mind. She ventured into the comfortable living room where her family had lived their lives ...until now. She sat down on the box-cluttered couch, and turned her face so that her vivid blue eyes could look deeply into her mother's eyes, which were a reflection of her own. She studied Leigh's drawn face. Had she taken the time to really look, she would have seen the pain and heartache that her mother was living through---but all Cassie allowed to register was the stern set jawline that had taken up permanent residence on Leigh's face since this nightmare had begun.

"Cassie, I know this seems like the end of the world to you, but this move is a Godsend for us." Leigh knew that her words were falling on deaf ears, but she didn't know what to say to her daughter to make her understand. "We have no other choice but to move where we can survive. God bless Granddad and Grandma for their loving gift." She glanced at her distraught daughter, not knowing what to say.

Leigh hesitated, then offered her hand to her daughter but then drew it back, rethinking the gesture. "You'll see," she said, "this is for the best—for all of us." Her smile didn't quite make it to her eyes. She knew her daughter was struggling with the move. How could life be this cruel?

Cassie watched as her mother physically struggled with their discussion. "Mom, you have been there for me all through my life. You are my rock. How can you tear my world apart? You are the only one that can save me now and you refuse to even think about other options." Cassie felt her heart break as a wave of sadness for this woman washed over her. She lowered her head so that her strawberry blonde hair hid the fleeting compassion she felt for her mother. Then the memories of what was coming came flooding into her mind. She stiffened. What was she thinking? Why was she defending her mother when she was intent on destroying her life?

She stared at the woman facing her with a hate that surprised her. Her mother's posture was rigid as she braced herself for another wave of her daughter's wrath. Cassie refused to acknowledge the weary look on Leigh's face. She wanted the mother she had loved and trusted for all of her fifteen years of life to return.

One thing she knew about her mom was that she was stubborn. And, although she seemed tired and beaten, she was unwavering in her decisions. When she got something in her mind, no one could sway her. She would stick by her convictions no matter what.

Cassie felt as if her head would spin off her shoulders. There had to be a way to get through Leigh's craziness and bring back the reasonable, loving mom she had known before their lives had been disassembled.

She willed her emotions to subside. "Mom, please, for once, I beg of you, back away from your decision. Please think about what you're doing to me . . . to us. Your life is here as much as mine. Please don't take us away from our home." She refused to cry any more tears. She had cried enough to make the toughest hard-ass change their minds. A monsoon of tears was not going to change her mother's decision.

It was too late. Her home belonged to someone else now. It had sold quickly. Cassie had hoped that the slow housing market would be in her favor. She knew that if she could keep the house from selling, then her mother would have to stay in Louisville, at least until it sold. But, par for her luck these days, the house sold within the first month of being on the market.

Cassie remembered watching as her broken mother began her trip downtown to Redfin Realtors' office. She was meeting with the "soon-to-be" new owners to sign the deed, giving away their home. Leigh had paused at the front door as if inspecting the house for clues of what had gone wrong in her idyllic life. She'd straightened her back, turned, and closed the door behind her.

Weeks later Cassie was still in shock that her mother had actually gone through with the sale. She glanced around the room and cringed at the sight of all the boxes stacked in every nook and cranny. Her only hope was to persuade her mother to stay in the city. They could get a smaller house; one that they could afford. Cassie didn't mind living in a smaller house as long as she was in her old neighborhood. She had pleaded this argument with her mother for days. She'd even searched the Courier-Journal and found three different houses for sell close to their neighborhood that were much smaller, but Leigh would have none of it. She even searched for rental property, but again her mother refused to discuss staying.

Frustrated and restless, Cassie couldn't sit still any longer. She rose from the couch and began pacing. What can I say that will cut through the stubbornness Mom has pulled around her? She looked at the shell of the woman that was her mother—a distraught and vacant stare glazed her eyes.

Cassie took up the argument once again. "I know all the reasons you say we need to move, Mom, but think about the reasons why we should stay."

Leigh drew in a deep breath and looked at her daughter, "I wish I could make living here happen for you, Cassie, but I know that we are supposed to leave here and start afresh. You don't realize it now, but this is best. We can start over; away from all of the heartache and turmoil."

Cassie, unable to come up with a different argument, begged one last time, "Please. Mom." The words caught in her throat. She felt her heart beating hard inside her chest. She wanted to shake her mother. Her eyes pierced Leigh with a look of despair and then panic as she pleaded, "Mom, just give it some time. If we can't make it here, then we can always go to Grandma and Granddad's house." Just saying the words made a chill wash over her.

As Cassie searched her mother's face, she realized that as anguished as her mother was, she had not changed her mind about moving to Eastern Kentucky.

Two

As Cassie opened her eyes, her face was red and sticky from the car window she had been using as a pillow. She gazed out of the face-imprinted window, watching the countryside roll past. This landscape was definitely different from home. She watched as tall hills, and mountains hugged the highway on each side of the car.

She felt herself smothering from the large monsters hovering over her. The mountainsides, spotted with struggling, spindly, cedar trees, formed steep walls that engulfed the highway. Loose dirt spilled from the slices cut in the rocky Appalachian Mountains. The rocks sliding from their resting spots on the mountain were encapsulating her in this place--with no way out. She couldn't believe she was actually moving here … to her 'new home.'

New home, yeah, right. What was her mother thinking? Why would anyone choose to live in this God forsaken place instead of their beautiful home in downtown Louisville? Why was her mother making her move away from everything she had ever known? She thought about the speech her mother had been repeating to her over and over again. If she heard her mother say one more time that this was a Godsend, because now they would have a free home; that moving here was the answer to their problems; she would scream. How could her mother take her from their home in historic Old Louisville and her friends she had been with since kindergarten at St. Mary's? What about her best friends, Jessica and Megan?

Because of her mother's stubbornness, she had to leave her life to come to this isolated countryside. This place with nothing but rocks, trees, hills, and fences around fields, that held lots of cows and horses. She watched as field after field of tobacco and corn, and something that looked like bean bushes (she wasn't sure what the plant was exactly) passed by her window, taking her closer to her great-grandparents' farm. The only time she had come to Magoffin County was when she'd spent a week with her great-grandparents. She had been nine. Yes, she would admit she'd loved helping her great-grandparents with the farm chores. She had loved the fields of corn, perfect for playing "hide and seek." She smiled as she remembered playing with her cousins while hiding among the large corn stalks that were taller than all three of them. But she didn't love it so much that she wanted to LIVE there. And even if she loved it, she had been nine years old. Now she was on the verge of adulthood and ready for her life to begin, not shut down back in the mountains.

Her thoughts drifted to the time she spent on the farm as a child. She remembered her great-granddad Sam taking her with him when he went to milk in the evening. He had allowed her to pull at the cow's teats, squeezing the milk free. A thin stream of milk had landed in the bucket. Granddad Sam had laughed and taken over the milking. He had aimed it toward her and shot her with a stream of warm milk. Both of them had laughed so hard that tears came to their eyes. Cassie's forehead creased; she knew she would miss Granddad Sam at the farm.

Grandma Lizzy had been just as much fun. She had taken Cassie with her to help gather the eggs from the chicken coop. It was scary to go into the coop with all the chicks staring at them as if they were egg thieves. Grandma had laughed at Cassie's fear. But, she'd made Cassie feel safe by talking her through collecting the eggs left by, 'their feathered friends.'

Cassie would always keep those wonderful memories from that summer long ago, but this time her visit to the farm would not be a fun vacation. Both grandparents had passed away, first Grandma Lizzy and then Granddad Sam. They had left their farm to their favorite granddaughter, Cassie's mother. The timing was awful. Cassie's parents, Leigh and Jack Ward had officially divorced, and she was certain this was the motivation behind her mother's insane decision to move them to this strange world—Howard Farm.

So, here they were with their belongings packed in the Explorer, along with the rented U-Haul tagging along behind, destined for the Howard Farm on Lick Creek Road, Salyersville, Kentucky.

Cassie stole a glance at her mother, driving with a smile of contentment on her face. How could she be so happy when she was destroying her only child's life? Did she divorce her reasoning along with Cassie's father? Had her mother even thought about what she was going to do, day after day, in this forsaken, uncivilized world?

They had always been close. Her mother had been her most devoted cheerleader. She was always there, like when her friends didn't show for her birthday party in second grade, or when she was scared to perform in the dance recital, or when she had succeeded in dancing in "The Nutcracker."

But now, when she faced the most devastating event in her life—the divorce of her parents, she felt alone. She couldn't go to her mom for support and comfort or advice on how to handle the situation. No, this time her mom was the cause of the problem. She had betrayed Cassie.

The highway was increasingly curvy—a sure sign that they were getting close to Magoffin County. Just when Cassie willed her eyes to watch the scenery, the Powell County welcoming sign zoomed into view. Okay, only one county left to go through, and then good ole Magoffin County ... population maybe 10,000. She had actually googled Magoffin County and discovered the population. If she had to live here she might as well know something about the place. She wondered if any of the 10,000 were young, or ancient like her great-grandparents. She didn't recall any people her age except her cousins visiting from Ohio during the same week she visited years ago. Cassie was sure that no one in his or her right mind would willingly agree to live in this place. Great, she would be living in the mountains, all alone without any friends, just old people. She felt the rocky hills pulling closer together as she moved farther and farther into the land of Eastern Kentucky.

As she thought of the life she so desperately didn't want, but seemed destined to endure, she became determined to think of happier things. She had good memories of the week she had spent on the farm those many years ago, but that was when Granddad and Grandma were there. And, she was nine years old at the time, her life was simple, and it didn't take much to make her happy: A bunch of animals, Granddad and his jokes, Grandma and her loving ways; that was a good time. But, now she was growing up and wanted to experience the world and see what it had to offer. Just when her life was starting to explode with possibilities, her mother had yanked her away. She gave her mom an exasperated look and changed the music on her iPod. At least she could get that to work. She'd checked her phone several times on the drive up the mountains—still no signal.

If her phone couldn't be used in this place how was she going to keep in contact with her friends and the real world? She stared down at her useless phone. Oh, how she wanted to talk with Megan and Jessica. Wonder what they're doing today? Missing me? They're probably hanging out at the gym, already forgetting me. I bet they go to 4th Street Live tonight while I sit around Grandma and Granddad's fireplace with my mother. She made a face at the reflection in the side window of the Explorer. It's going to be a fun weekend for me. She winced at the sarcastic thought. I just hope that it is the only weekend spent with my mother.

She shivered. What was it about that house that made her skin crawl? She vaguely remembered a weird experience during her visit six years ago, but obviously it wasn't too significant because she couldn't remember what happened. Still, when she thought of the farmhouse she had a weird sensation that she could describe only as fear and dread. Why would she fear Granddad and Grandma Howard's home? They had been so nice to her. They made her feel comfortable. So, why did she have prickly skin every time she allowed herself to think of living in that house? Was it just because she wanted to be in her home, in her room, in her bed, living her life? That had to be it; there could be no other explanation.

Cassie allowed her eyes to scan the highway. Where were they right now? They had been traveling for at least three and a half hours, and according to her mom's GPS they were probably near Morgan County, which was next door to Magoffin County. Cassie stole a look at her mom. She had a pasted smile on her face that told Cassie that she was still in the world of bliss.

She knew her mother was hurting from the divorce-- she had done everything to keep the family together. Cassie still refused to believe her father was as bad as he seemed. She knew he was sick. According to everything she had read, alcohol and drugs were sicknesses. She could not blame her father for being sick. She had to believe that he would get better at the rehab center he'd checked himself into a month ago. But their lives would never be the same. He had walked away from Cassie and her mother and married another woman ... the woman that Cassie blamed for all his problems. He would never have gotten sick with drugs and alcohol if she hadn't attached herself to him.

The only time Cassie really got mad and stressed about her father was when his habits had caused her mom to lose their home in order to pay off her dad's debts. Her mother never discussed the amount, but she was upset a lot lately. She had overheard her mom talking with her friends and knew that her father was spending lots of money every day ... hence, no other choice but to sell away their lives and come to Magoffin to live in a free house her mother had inherited. Cassie felt a small amount of guilt for feeling resentment for her great-grandparents' generous act.

She looked up and out of her side window to see the "Welcome to Magoffin County" sign passing. Her heart got a little weak; it was not going to be long now. Her mom turned from her driving long enough to take Cassie's hand and give it a small squeeze, offering a faint smile. "We're almost home sweetie. Please give it a chance. This move could be a new and exciting opportunity for us, Cass."

Was she serious? Cassie refused to give her the smile she knew her mother needed. She would not make this easy. She fought the urge to pull her hand away and plead one more time to stay in Louisville.

But, she knew they had come this far and shortly, they would find their way to Granddad's farm; and, if her mother had anything to do with it, never to return to Cassie's wonderful life again. How would she survive for three years, while she waited to turn 18 and leave this God forsaken land? Was it time to face her nightmare? Moments passed, and her mom gave the signal to turn onto exit 75, for downtown Salyersville.

As she took in the sights, she saw roofing tin being used as fence walls that hid most, but not all of the wrecked and rusted cars in the lot on the right side of the street. Across the street, sat the well-groomed Magoffin Board of Education building. This is it, the town of Salyersville … soon to be her hometown. She would never call this place home.

There didn't seem to be many businesses in the town, and so far, only one stoplight. As her mom continued driving, Cassie surveyed her surroundings. She saw an old brick building with a painted front window, announcing Pam's V&S Variety Store. The other side of the building sported a Thrift Shop" sign, and across the street sat a large building with white columns making it look as if it had come from the Civil War era—the sign read, "Licking River Baptist Church." Straight ahead were more of the rock-covered mountains. They were a little scary for her. What if those rocks decided to tumble down to the roadside? People could get hurt, and by people she meant her.

Cassie's mom brought her back to reality by announcing each section of town: three pharmacies, the public library, community center, and then, another stop light. "Wow. Two stop lights." As she looked to her left, she saw The Salyersville National Bank and the U.S. Post Office. Her mom turned the opposite direction, leaving Cassie to face Speedway, Brenda's Hair Salon, Town and

Country Flowers, and Caudill's Feed and Supply. Cassie smiled; remembering that this store had been Granddad's favorite. She had gone into town with him when he needed to buy some feed and medicine for the animals, and they had stopped at Caudill's Feed and Supply.

She had felt so important because her Granddad had asked her to go shopping with him. Going with him had been much more fun than playing outside with Barry and Deb.

When they walked into the store, Mark, the owner, had shouted Granddad's name as if he were his best friend, and Granddad had done the same to him. Cassie remembered the sense of ease and contentment she'd felt. Were all of its citizens as friendly and welcoming as Mark had been? Just one big happy family. That would be easy if you were old … thirty, or something, when you had determined your life's path already. But Cassie was fifteen and her life was just getting started, not winding down. Her plans didn't include being best friends with the local feed store owner. As far as she knew there were no people in this place even near her age. When she was nine, her cousins had come to stay at Grandma's and Granddad's the same week she stayed. Yes, it had been a fun week, but Barry and Deb would not be living here now … just her by herself.

Cassie's mom interrupted her thoughts, "Almost there. I remember driving this curvy road when I was sixteen and trying to beat my curfew. Mom was always waiting up, so I knew there would be trouble when I came in the door." Leigh sighed, "No sneaking out late for me."

Leigh sneaked a peak at her daughter, "Cassie, you are going to LOVE living here. Salyersville is a great town. We don't have to worry about the dangers you faced in the city. Just good people living good lives."

"Right Mom, just what I want, a bunch of old farts that don't know what having fun is when it hits them on their butts. I wonder if there's anyone my age IN THIS TOWN." And to herself she added, "And do I want to be friends with anyone that is weird enough to live in this town?"

Cassie's mom smiled and said, "You'll find lots of friends, Cassie, give it a chance." She took a quick but loving look at her daughter and pulled her attention back to the curving road. The effects of the mountains were already happening. Country music was on every radio station. Oh well, back to her iPod. Between the iPod and hopefully the iPhone, she would have enough power to stay connected to the real world and this twilight zone of a town would not suck her into its weirdness. There was just so much of Reba and Toby Keith a person could listen to and still be sane.

How long did they have to travel this road before getting to the farm? How far away from town were they? Not that Salyersville accounted for a town, but still, how far? She watched small, boxed houses as they passed by the window. One after the other, she saw similar things: porches, animals in the front yard, vegetable gardens set to the sides of the houses, vehicles sitting in front of the homes. This was it? Was her mom determined to destroy her life, so that she could live in this PLACE?

Finally, they were turning onto another road. Set in the corner of the adjoining roads rested a BP gas station. It seemed to be busy. Parked in front of the gas station were pickup trucks, jeeps, and large trucks with horses being hauled behind, motorcycles, and two of those tiny vehicles that everyone in Salyersville wanted. Granddad called them "mules." He said they worked better than four-wheelers when traveling over the hills. Apparently they were being put to the test, although she saw at least five four-wheelers sitting in front of the station.

Before she knew it, she had marveled out loud, "those could be fun to ride."

"They are. Uncle Ray bought one to use on his farm. He says they are incredible for checking fence rows around the property and then just to have fun riding."

Oh no, Mom, you will not get back in that easily. Cassie felt her mind shouting in her head. She had stolen her life from her; no way could she assume she was just going to have a casual conversation. Cassie's plan was to wear her mom down until she would relent and take her back to the city where they both belonged.

The road was becoming curvier and narrower than before. How were two cars supposed to pass each other? Evidently, the locals had mastered it because as her mom inched along, the other cars were whizzing past her. They both winced each time they felt the wind from a passing vehicle. Cassie guessed her mom had been away long enough that driving on these roads was as unsettling for her, as it was for Cassie.

As Cassie was settling in for the last leg of the trip, her mom put on her signal for another right turn. Not another winding road to nowhere, she thought. This one was practically a one-lane road. Cassie struggled to hide her emotions.

OMG, coming down the country road were three horses with riders. Was this a normal event? What would be next, a covered wagon? Would the Indians swoop down to scalp them? As they came closer, Cassie discovered that these riders were young people riding horses. Not only were they boys, but cute boys that were her age. She felt her heart begin to beat a little quicker. They were here—in this place? Maybe they live around here. They look normal, other than the fact that they were riding horses down a highway.

Her mom, who was already driving slowly, slowed down even more. It was a little embarrassing, but at least she got a good look at the three riders. Good looking. All three had strong muscled bodies, and one had the nicest blonde, almost white, hair with the clearest blue eyes that looked straight into hers and made her blush in spite of herself. He smiled, showing gleaming white even teeth. She looked away, to find herself looking into another cute face. His smile gave way to the most adorable dimples that made his face look chiseled like those men you see in Abercrombie commercials. The other one, just as cute with his dark eyes and hair, leaned down and spoke through the open car window. She tried to breathe evenly while he was so close to her. "Hey, glad to meet the two of you.

23

Welcome to Lick Creek. Are you the ladies moving to the Howard farm?"

Trying desperately to keep her mind on the conversation, she kept wondering if her hair and face were presentable. She had just spent hours sleeping on the hard surface of her window. She tried to focus on what he was saying through the half opened window.

He was welcoming them to the Creek; did that mean he lived here? Were they to be neighbors? No, she could not be that lucky.

While pulling the car window down in order to have a conversation, Leigh answered, "Why, yes we are. How did you know about us? Do I know you?"

The dark haired boy smiled, "Sorry, I'm Josh … My mom, Anita, is your friend?"

"Anita's son. Josh." Leigh searched the boy's face and smiled. "It's so good to see you."

"Mom's excited about your coming to Lick Creek to live. It's all we've discussed at my house since she found out."

Leigh smiled, "You look different now that you aren't in diapers!" Leigh giggled. "It's been a while. Tell Anita I'm expecting to see her soon."

"Who are your friends? Do I know their families too?" Leigh looked at the other two boys. They didn't look like any of the boys she had gone to school with, but you never knew.

Josh motioned to the blonde boy, "This is Seth, and he lives on Bloomington Road, not far from here. His dad is John Barnett. They moved here probably after you moved away." Leigh smiled at the boy, and he returned the smile while sneaking a peek at Cassie that was obvious to all except Cassie. Josh nodded his head toward the other boy and introduced him as Jake, another friend from Buffalo Creek.

"Good to meet you boys," Leigh smiled and looked at Cassie for her greeting.

She caught Cassie off guard, and the result was a stuttered, "Hi, I'm Cassie." The boys smiled approvingly and nodded.

As her mom nodded her goodbye, she drove up the road and began laughing. "Pull your eyes back into your head little girl and close your mouth."

Cassie turned to look her mother in the eyes. "Who were they; do you know?"

"I know Josh lives on the farm next to ours. His mother is Anita, you remember my best friend from high school? The other boys live near here if they live on Bloomington and Buffalo. I guess you could say they are our neighbors." Leigh smiled. "What do you think?"

"Sounds like it," Cassie mumbled deeply in shock. The fact that these boys were her neighbors was too good to be true. Wait until she told Jessica and Megan. They would never believe this. Three … not one … not two … but three beautiful specimens of men had just fallen from the sky into this forgotten world. Okay, one plus for this place, not enough to make her happy, but a plus.

Cassie noticed her mom getting fidgety. Was she tired from driving or anxious to get to the house? Cassie was feeling a tug at her heart for her mom. This move had to be hard for her too. She had lived in Louisville for the past twenty years. It would have to be difficult for her to come back here to live. Wonder how many of the people in this town knew about her father and the divorce? Cassie's empathy didn't last long. She snapped back when her thoughts reminded her that she didn't have to come here; they could have made it in Louisville.

Her mom interrupted her thoughts with, "Look Cassie, our land. This land on both sides of the road belongs to you and me—we are home."

Cassie didn't want to look. If she looked, she would have to acknowledge the fact that she was moving here… living here … rotting here … ugh. She made no comment to her mother. She pretended to be fixing her iPod while her mom exclaimed about the pastures, the fields, and the land. Finally, the car began to slow down and her mom parked in front of a house that looked as if it came from a "Gone with the Wind" movie set.

Three

Cassie sucked in her breath, just as her mom allowed hers to release. She had that squirrelly feeling again. Why did she feel so anxious when she thought of this house? She turned to get a good look at the farmhouse. If she looked hard enough, she could almost see Granddad and Grandma sitting in the wooden rockers on the front porch. On the other side of the porch, rested the swing she and her cousins had used every day during that week so long ago. The porch looked the same except the paint on the chairs was chipping away and the metal chain that held the swing was brown with rust. The worn porch floor guided them from the stone steps to the large screened door.

Looking at the house sent goose bumps down her spine. Was she afraid she would see her great-grandparents? She smiled a sad smile, no; she was afraid because she knew they wouldn't be here. They would never be here again. This house was the epitome of them and the thought of living here without them was making her sad. Her heart hurt worse now than the day her mom had broken the news to her that Granddad Sam was gone.

She looked wistfully toward the house, "Oh, Grandma Lizzy, I miss you so much. Who'll fix those wonderful country meals you use to make for me?" Not her mom, she was strictly a boxed food cook. She pictured her Granddad walking across the road to the barn to milk the cows. Now who would take her on walks over the pasture and teach her to milk? Tears began pushing at Cassie's eyelids. No, she would not allow her mom the pleasure of seeing her cry for this house. She refused to give her any reason to think she was ready to make her great-grandparents' farm her home. This place would never be home to her.

She glanced back at her mom and saw an anxious look on her mother's face that she was not prepared to see. She looked flushed and pale at the same time. This panic and tension wasn't like her mother at all; she was always cool and at ease in any situation. What was her mother thinking that would make her look like this? Well, whatever it was, Cassie refused to ask her about it. As far as she was concerned, her mother's thoughts could be kept to herself, and she in return would keep hers to herself. She knew that would make her mother miserable. "Good," she said quietly.

Leigh saw Cassie looking at her, and she shook her face free of the emotions that had caused her anxiety. "We're home—let's go check it out."

Cassie was beginning to believe that her mom was as nervous as she was about being in this house. As Cassie realized this she began thinking about her mom. These were her grandparents, and they loved her enough to give her their home and all their earthly wealth. Of course, she was going to be emotional. Cassie's heart went out to her mom. Yes, she was angry, but she didn't want her mother to have to go through any more misery. The last year was enough; her dad had taken care of that. She reached over and gave her a hug. "Let's do it, Mom. But I'm still not agreeing to live here. I want to go home. Just so you know."

Her mom hugged her back. "Just give it a chance, please Cassie?" She reached up and gave Cassie's hair a tug. Something her mom had always done when being affectionate with her. Cassie smiled back and turned toward the screened door and gave a push. As they entered, Cassie felt frigid air pass by her. Odd, it's the end of summer and freezing air was trapped in the house. How did that happen?

Cassie and her mom looked at each other with a look of "what was that?" Neither spoke out loud of what had just occurred. Instead, Cassie's mom pulled her forward, the two of them holding hands. Cassie didn't refuse; this was the eeriest thing she had ever experienced. As they stepped into the front room, the first thing Cassie saw was her granddad's rocking chair he sat in after lunch, while he read his bible. She could still see him in her mind's eye, sitting in that chair reading as he rubbed the smooth wood on the arm of the chair. He would often rest his elbows on the worn wooden arm as he told her not-so-funny jokes. His 'end-table', as Grandma called it, sat nudged between the wall and the rocker. A large boxed radio sat on top of the small table. Cassie could still see Granddad's fingertip smudges on the tuning dial. The ancient black rotary phone was still resting beside the radio. Seeing the phone made her smile. Even though the phone was next to Granddad's chair, he never answered any calls. He didn't hear well and refused to admit that it was his loss of hearing that made telephone conversations difficult for him and for the caller. When the phone rang, Grandma would clip through the house on her swollen feet to answer the phone. With thirteen children, the phone rang a lot.

Watching Grandma talk on the phone had been one of Cassie's funniest memories. Grandma positioned the black receiver next to her ear, but the mouthpiece always ended up on her nose. She would shout into the phone and complain that her phone just didn't work right, but Cassie had told her "if you pull this part down Grandma, it will make your voice louder and they can hear you better." She'd agreed that might be the problem and vowed to pull the receiver down the next time. Each time she agreed, she would get another phone call and every time the receiver ended up resting on her nose.

She would push Granddad up from his throne, pick up the phone, rest the mouthpiece on her nose, and shout as she talked. Granddad would watch her face, anxious to hear that the kids and grandkids were okay. Cassie smiled at the memory. She turned to her mom, and her mom whispered, "This is so them."

Cassie nodded. "Yes it is."

As the two got control of their emotions, Granddad's radio, still tuned to a local radio station, began blaring the farm report. The two jumped and stopped in their tracks. Cassie finally reminded herself to breathe. Leigh shook off her fear and nervously laughed. "Well, looks like the radio is excited to have company." She walked over to the small side table and twisted the wooden knob on the radio to the "off" position. They both released their breath but before Leigh could return to Cassie's side, the phone began to ring. She paused and then picked up the receiver. "Hello." No answer. "Must have been a wrong number." She replaced the antique receiver but before she could walk away, it began to ring again. She answered, but no one was on the other end. Without looking at her daughter, she replaced the receiver and rushed back to Cassie. Just as she grabbed Cassie's hand, the radio began blaring. Cassie was frozen in position. Leigh moved quickly to turn off the radio.

Cassie was beginning to understand why she was having an eerie feeling of dread and anxious tension whenever this house was involved. They hadn't been in the house for more than an hour, and already weird things were happening. Shouldn't her great-grandparents' house have warm fuzzy feelings for her? When she'd visited, Grandma and Granddad had made her time in this house a happy time. She couldn't remember any scary moments that had occurred during her stay, but, as far as she was concerned, today's episodes were enough to explain why she felt apprehension.

Wanting the feelings of fear to end, Cassie made her legs work and followed her mother. They walked around the room surveying her great-grandparent's possessions. The furniture was worn from years of use but gave the two a sense that a part of Grandma was still with them.

The ceilings of the old house were high, and the woodwork that surrounded the wall was as beautiful as ever. Cassie's eyes came to rest on the old fireplace. Grandma had told her stories about the fireplace. Stories of Cassie's Grandpa Bill, her mom's dad, popping home-grown corn by holding large pans over the fire and shaking them back and forth until the steam built up inside the kernel and it exploded. They also grew their own peanuts and sweet potatoes, roasting them in the fire grate. Cassie remembered that faraway look on her grandmother's face when she'd talk about how they would spend their days.

She also remembered that some of Grandma's stories had left her fearful of the fireplace. She told of once, turning around to find that her son Raymond had backed so close to the fire trying to get warm that he caught his pants on fire. The older boys had grabbed him and rolled him in a rug placed in front of the hearth.

There were also stories that made the family uneasy. She spoke of a burst of fire that would roll out of the opening of the fireplace for no apparent reason. She had described the fireballs as big as watermelons and would move from one side of the fireplace to the other as if searching for something. Grandma would get quiet for a moment, thinking, or perhaps visualizing the fire in her mind. From what Grandma Lizzy said, this occurred all the time she lived in the house. Grandma Lizzy had told these stories without any fear in her voice. Even so, they scared Cassie.

One evening, during her visit those many years ago, Cassie had sat in the big room while her great uncles and aunts came to visit. They all began discussing the house as if the strange things that happened in the house were entertainment. She had listened closely and their stories had left her with fear of the fireplace. It dominated the house. It was not only in the living room but the opposite side was in her great-grandparents' bedroom and also in the dining room downstairs. Upstairs the fireplace was open to two different bedrooms. The large ornate mantles and hearths gave the house a formal, elegant style. As she stared in amazement, she realized that now these eerie fireplaces belonged to her mother and her.

Maybe her thoughts were showing on her face because her mom pushed her past the domineering fireplace and into the dining room. Welcoming them was the opening of yet another fireplace with a large buffet that Grandma had pushed against the front opening. Her grandma used the buffet to store her glass pie plates, cake holders, pitchers and drinking glasses. It was an area in Grandma's house that had amazed Cassie. The wood on the buffet was carved and heavy. It was an expensive piece of furniture. The buffet fit well in the house. One afternoon, while Grandma had been busy cleaning the kitchen from the lunch meal, Cassie asked her about the beautiful cabinet. Grandma had dismissed it with a wave of her hand and said, "Oh, that old thing was left here when we moved in the house. It was so large and heavy that I just left it, and I use it to set my sweets on."

Everything looked the same as she remembered. The old Frigidaire refrigerator stood in the corner where it had always been. The refrigerator door stood open. It was unplugged. Cassie guessed that someone had come in and unplugged all the electrical appliances, probably after Granddad had passed away. The dining table was still in the same spot with the chairs pushed close, as if waiting for Grandma and Granddad to sit down and have their lunch. It was metal with vinyl seat cushions in white and yellow to match the top of the table. Cassie had seen similar dining tables and chairs in the antique shops her mom had dragged her to during her decorating frenzy. Looking at Grandma Lizzy's table and chairs made the ones in the shop look hard and fake. Grandma's table and chairs were real and welcoming. Probably because of all the good food Grandma had served on them throughout the years.

Cassie could see Grandma's face smiling at her while she told her to "eat that honey; it won't hurt you." Even if you didn't like greens, she made them sound good. Cassie smiled at the memory. Maybe living in this house would be comforting—or not.

Moving on to the kitchen, Cassie and her mom stood still looking at the old farm stove and remembering Grandma cooking day after day, creating mouth-watering food. They could see her stirring the pots on top of the stove. Cassie turned to her mom and said, "I miss her," and her mom looked back with tears threatening to spill over. Leigh nodded her head in agreement.

How were these two novice cooks going to use this stove, an artist's instrument, and feel okay about the pathetic plates of food they would produce. When Cassie expressed this to her mom they both giggled and for a fleeting moment, things were okay with the two of them again.

The house had only one bathroom--less than adequate for the two girls that were used to having separate bathrooms. "How is this going to work, Mom? There is no way we can both use this room."

"We can for a while. I'll have Uncle Ray find someone to fix it up and maybe put another one in the back bedroom." Cassie had that all too familiar shiver when her mom mentioned the back bedroom. Why? She couldn't put her finger on it, but something didn't feel right with that room. She was scared of the room but didn't know why. It just wasn't like Cassie to be afraid. She was never scared of the dark or of being alone.

Her mom interrupted her thoughts, "Ready to go upstairs?"

"I guess." She could have left the upstairs alone for a while. The chills came again. As they made their way up the back stairs each stair step creaked as their weight settled. Each tread made its own particular sound. Cassie fought the impulse to turn and run back down. Instead, she followed her mom up the remaining stairs and opened the door that led to the suite of bedrooms. The first room was large and open. It looked like a princess hide-a-way. The windows were wide allowing light to flood the room. The next room looked like a powder room. It was unusual because the fireplace that dominated the center of the house downstairs made its way up here, as well. Maybe this space had been used as a sitting room for the lady of the house.

Cassie brought her imagination back to reality. "Mom, who's sleeping here? Will this be my room? Will you sleep in Grandma and Granddad's bedroom?" Cassie couldn't stop her rambling. She knew her mother would think this was the room Cassie would want. But for some unknown reason, Cassie was scared she'd end up in this room with all of her chills and goose bumps.

Her mom frowned. "I haven't thought that far ahead. I don't think I want to sleep in Grandma and Granddad's room. Where do you want to sleep?"

"Not the back bedroom."

Her mom laughed, "Okay, you decide where you want, and I'll take what's left, deal?"

"Deal. Only I don't want any of these rooms." She faced her mother, "Mom; they give me the willies."

Leigh bit her lip, a sure sign that she was nervous, "It's just because we're used to Granddad and Grandma being here. You know they wanted us to live here. They gave us their home as a gift of their love." She smiled while raising her chin, "I have decided I will sleep in their beautiful four poster bed. I think that's what they'd want."

"Then, I'll try this room." Cassie said, pushing the fear and dread away. It was a beautiful room, why wouldn't she like it? She was giving in to the wild imagination of a girl that had been reading too many suspense thrillers. This house had belonged to Granddad and Grandma, not some ax murderer.

Cassie's mom gave her a nudge. "Let's get our things from the car. We might as well make it our own." As she turned to leave, Cassie lunged toward the door, not wanting to be left in the room alone.

If she couldn't be left for a second in her new room without her "mommy", then how on earth was she going to spend every night, and as her mom said, 'make it her own space?' She didn't want to be alone for a moment in this room or any of the rooms. That was it; this was not her home. This house was not her mother's home; it belonged to her grandparents. Couldn't Mom see that? This house would never be theirs. Maybe the house was trying to tell them. Maybe that is why she had such eerie feelings. Listen to me. I have gone crazy. If Jessica and Megan could hear me, they would laugh themselves silly.

Speaking of Jessica and Megan, wonder if my phone will have a signal from here? Cassie made her way down the creaking stairway into the comfy living room. She scooted out the front door and to the car pulling her phone and iPod out of the front seat. Pushing Jessica's number, she heard the ringing and then "YES." It was Jessie's voice.

"Jessica, is that you? Thank God. I was beginning to think that I would never hear from my friends ever again."

"Hey, Cassie. Where are you? Have you persuaded your mom to come home yet? We miss you."

"I miss you guys so much. I just got here, and no, Mom has not changed her mind. She's determined to make me stay here. Jessica, it's spooky to walk through their house without them here. I feel spooked when I go upstairs and into the back bedrooms. Silly, huh?"

"What is going on there, Cassie? You sound funny." There was silence for a moment and then, "Are you okay, girl?"

"I'm fine. Just wanting to come home. I'll be okay." Cassie remembered the boys on horses, "Oh, Jessica, you guys won't believe what happened on our way to the house. There were three gorgeous boys riding horses down the road from where my great-grandparents' farm is located. I couldn't keep my eyes from bulging out. You have to see. My mom says that they are our neighbors. One of them is even my next door neighbor."

As she began walking down the large rocks that formed the walkway to the porch, she heard the sound of a honking horn. She turned to see her mom's Uncle Ray in his red pickup truck. She said a quick goodbye to Jessica and turned to greet her great uncle.

"Hey, are you the pretty girls moving in the neighborhood?" He laughed as Cassie's mom leaped toward him for a hug. In one smooth move, he was out of the truck and hugging Leigh. He turned and motioned to Cassie to give him a hug and she obliged. She remembered Uncle Ray from her visit years ago, but barely. She thought she liked him. He was trying his best to welcome them. "Would you girls like to come over to my house for some supper? Betty is fixing a celebration dinner to welcome you to your new home."

Cassie wanted to scream. This was not her new

home. She did not feel like celebrating but she was hungry, so she looked at her mom and smiled. "Please Mom."

"I'd love to see Aunt Betty," Leigh offered.

Uncle Ray motioned them both into his pickup and pulled away from the huge white house. Cassie felt a wave of relief. How odd that her grandparents' house made her feel this way. It had to be because her mother was forcing her to stay in their house pretending it was her own. And, the incident with the radio and phone hadn't helped. As the radio and phone occurrence flashed in her mind, she felt anger and fear flow into her throat once again. She had to think of something else. She would think of the good food that awaited her at Aunt Betty's.

When Uncle Ray pulled in his driveway, Aunt Betty, a short, chubby middle-aged lady, was standing in the door, waving. Right out of the Ladies Home Journal, apron and all. "Are you girls hungry? I told Ray; those girls have had a long drive today and need some good food. I hope you like fried chicken."

"Sounds good to me." Cassie was hungry. It had been a long day, and she was ready to relax and have some good country cooking.

"Thank you Aunt Betty, this is so good of you." Leigh offered.

During dinner, Betty looked at Ray and then at Leigh. "Leigh, you've been gone a long time from the farm. What do you remember about life out here?"

"Not much, Aunt Betty. But, Cassie and I are ready for a change and what better place to make that happen than with the people who love us."

Ray gave his wife a stern look, "That is so true, Leigh. I want you to remember that we are here for you." He reached across the table and gave Leigh's hand a quick squeeze, "Anything you need, you just ask."

"Thanks, Uncle Ray."

"Your daddy was my big brother; he was always there for me. I can't think of anything that he would want me to do more than to look after his little girl." Uncle Ray said. His eyes glistened.

"You two are brave girls to be staying in that house," announced Aunt Betty.

"What do you mean?" Cassie quizzed. She could feel her skin begin to crawl. Uncle Ray cleared his throat and gave Betty a look that said, "Don't you dare."

Aunt Betty mumbled, "Nothing. It's just now with your grandparents gone; it will be lonely. Can't help but think of them when you are around their things all the time." Again, Uncle Ray cleared his throat, louder this time.

Cassie could feel the events of the day weigh down on her. She was ready to lie down and sleep, wherever that had to be. If the creepy bedroom that was now hers had a problem with that, it would have to wait until after she rested. Because now, she was going to sleep and hopefully have a better perspective of the situation when she woke.

Leigh noticed the tired face of her daughter and stood. "Betty, allow us to help clean your kitchen and then we must get back to the house. It has been a long day, and we need to get ourselves situated and get a good night's sleep."

"I won't hear of it. You go along and get yourselves ready for bed." She quickly began stacking the dishes as if showing off her skill for cleaning the kitchen. "I have these dishes; there will be plenty of more times for you to help." She brushed her chubby hand at them in a dismissal.

Back at home, Cassie crawled into the large bed without a thought and slept, a long deep sleep.

Four

Cassie opened one and then another eye to the sun beaming through the window. At first, she was confused as to where the sun was coming from and where she was. Then it all came tumbling in on her; she was at her "new" residence…Lick Creek Road. She closed her eyes and tried to go back to sleep. If she could sleep the next three years away, she'd go home by herself, and her mother could have this creepy old house. After a moment of silence, she determined that her wishing didn't work. She opened her eyes again to find she was still in her new sunlit bedroom.

The room was pleasantly quiet and she had made it through the night without anything weird happening. That was a plus. Yesterday was a tiring day. That is why her imagination was running wild. This house was just a house, and this room was just a room, a nice room at that. She listened more intently and thought she heard her mother moving around downstairs. Might as well face the day and her mother's bright and sunny face. Ugh.

Cassie crept down the stairs, finding her mom in the master bedroom taking the bed linen off her bed. "Cassie, we need to make this house ours. Let's decorate. I know Grandma and Granddad would want us to make this house into a home that will make us comfortable and happy. I unpacked the bedding from home and thought we could start with changing our bedrooms. I stacked yours behind the stairs. Want help carrying it upstairs?"

"No, I can do it." Cassie's heart sank. This comforter was all that remained of her old bedroom. The reality of her fleeting life choked her. All she had left was memories. Memories of her mom and dad and the great life she had lived before the "Dad Meltdown." She climbed back up the stairs to remove Grandma's bedding and replace it with her own; from the bed she had slept in all her life. Just as she entered the bedroom, she felt a quick shove on her back. It was forceful enough that she fell forward. Luckily the bedding braced the fall. What had pushed her? She had not tripped, and the bedding wasn't that heavy. She looked around the room but found nothing different. How odd. She picked herself up from the floor and heard her mom calling. "Cassie, are you okay? I heard something fall."

"I'm fine, Mom. I must have tripped on the stairs as I came to the door." She knew that wasn't what happened, yet, what could she say? She didn't have a clue what had happened, but she knew something had pushed her. "I'm taking the bedding off and putting my old stuff on now."

"Can't wait to see how different the room looks, once we get things changed." Cassie looked around the room. How was this going to become her room? She felt as if it belonged to someone else, and she was a trespasser. She didn't feel welcome but she couldn't explain her feelings.

Grandma would have wanted her to make it her room. Mom was right about that. What was it about this room? She stayed as long as she could take the feeling of eeriness and finally decided she had to get some air. She'd had enough of this house. If she stayed any longer, she felt the house would chew her up and spit her out. She might as well help it out and find her way outside. She finished making her bed in her old floral bedding and was amazed that she felt nothing. She called down to her mom, "I think I want to do some exploring around the farm." She waited for her mother to comment but didn't get a response. "I'll be back a little later, okay." She heard a mumble from the back bedroom. She could tell her mother was on a mission with Grandma's house. Mixing the old with the new, that was mom's motto.

Cassie loved the comfort and modern style of their home in Louisville. She hadn't thought of what her mom had done to make their house beautiful. She could only imagine what Grandma Lizzy and Granddad Sam's house would look like a month from now.

Cassie bounced out of the house and breathed a free

and easy breath. She felt this was the first decent breath she had taken since she had entered the house yesterday. As she surveyed her surroundings, she heard her mother's voice from the day before telling her that all of this belonged to them. The fields that hugged the back lawn and circled around to the side yard then followed the highway for miles toward town. On the other side of the property, the pasture bordered the highway and ran as far as the eye could see. Huge black barns with red roofs rested in the center of the pastures across the road from the house. She wondered if there were any horses or cows in the pastures around the barns.

Cassie decided to take a long walk. She crossed the pebbled road leading to the barns and headed toward the stream and flat land beyond. This oasis was a vivid memory because she and her cousins had played there while they visited with their great-grandparents. On one particular day they had sneaked tobacco from one of the barns and made homemade cigarettes. It had been a disaster. They all got so sick they were green. Granddad swore that Grandma had poisoned them with lunch. Poor Grandma had taken the blame. No one ever found out they were just trying to be cool and smoke a cigarette.

Before she knew it, she was standing in front of the little stream and a large oak tree they had sat under all those years ago. The pasture seemed smaller now than six years ago. The tree even seemed to have shrunk. She smiled, maybe the tree hadn't shrunk but she had grown larger since she had last been there. She sat down under the tree and pulled her shoes off to rest her bare feet in the cool stream. It may seem smaller than she remembered, but it was relaxing. She sat back resting against the trunk of the tree wondering what she was going to do. How could she give up her life and stay in this place until she was eighteen? Because when she turned eighteen, she was leaving; she was going back to Louisville. She would live with her dad or get her own place.

Maybe she would go to school at The University of Louisville. The thought of being with her friends again made her smile. That is if she still had her friends. She hadn't heard from Megan, and the call to Jessica hadn't made her feel comfortable. What were they up to? Would they forget her now that she was so far away? Oh, how she wanted to go home. She closed her eyes and drifted off to sleep.

The next thing she knew she awakened with someone breathing very close to her neck. It startled her. Why would anyone get close enough that she could feel their breath? Her eyes flew open as she braced herself to confront her intruder. The only thing she found was the sun shining and a small breeze. The stream was making the only noise in the quiet paradise. But she KNEW that someone or something had blown their hot breath on her neck.

What was this? First, someone pushed her and now she was feeling someone breathing down her neck. Was she so homesick she was going crazy? She felt the goose bumps begin to grow on her skin. She slowly raised herself off the ground and carefully looked around the flat field and stream. She glanced up the hill that led to the fence line of the property and for a fleeting second she thought she saw a woman moving through the trees. She steadied her nerves and peered through the trees again. This time she found nothing out of the ordinary. There was nothing around except the birds and the minnows in the stream. Enough meditation. She made her way back across the meadow, toward the barns. As she walked back she had the strangest feeling. It felt as if someone was following her.

She tried to push the feeling aside; wondering how long had she been sleeping. She didn't have a watch and hadn't felt the need to keep track of the time. She must have been asleep for a long time if she had been so deeply asleep that her dream seemed real. Man, she must have been more tired from yesterday's trip than she realized. As she thought about what had happened in the field, she picked up speed. This farm was giving her the creeps, and she didn't like it one bit.

The farm was beautiful. She would enjoy a vacation

here. But what she was feeling at the moment wasn't the anger she had brought to the farm; it was anxious dread. She shook the feeling off when she came into the clearing and saw the barns resting against the hilly pasture. She made her way back to the pebbled road and noticed that her mom was on the front porch with a measuring tape and notepad. "What is that woman up to now?" mumbled Cassie.

She strolled up to the porch, watching her mom measure the wooden chairs and swings. She measured and then wrote the measurements on the small note pad. There was a crease between her brows, a sign that she was deep in thought. Leigh glanced up to see her daughter standing in front of her.

"What are you up to, Mom?"

"Making the porch look more like a part of this century. What do you think of black for the furniture with green paisley cushions? I think redbrick color for the floor."

Okay, her mom had found her hobby already. Fixing this house would keep her mind off of her ex-husband and his new bride. Unfortunately, Cassie found it difficult to forget. She didn't have a problem in forgiving him for his drinking and drug problem, but when he left them for this woman.... Cassie was finding it hard to face him. Their family was permanently broken. She felt that empty feeling building up inside of her. She had to think of something else.

"Mom, what am I supposed to do while we are here?" She refused to say while they live here. Her mom looked up with a sad wishful glance.

She held her daughter's eyes for just a moment. "You, my dear, will be in school—it starts in two days." Cassie could have sunk to the floor. She had not even thought of school. Of course, her mother would expect her to go to school. Going to school wasn't an option; she would have to go to school. She just could not bring herself to believe she would have to attend school in this little town of nowhere.

Where was a school? She had never seen one. OMG,

would she have to ride the bus? Could this get any worse? Okay, she took that back. There was no need to push fate. Did she dare ask her mom how she would be getting to school? She decided she would find out where the school was located—then she could worry about riding the bus.

Cassie watched without seeing as her mother pretended to be busy. Leigh was trying desperately to distract her daughter and derail her from an angry confrontation.

"Mom, do you know where the high school is? I've never even seen a school here." Cassie held her breath while waiting for her mom to tear her heart out just a little bit more.

"It's about six miles away, going towards town." Leigh paused, giving Cassie time to process what she was saying. "I asked my old friend Anita that lives up the road if her son, Josh, would mind picking you up on his way to school. That way you don't have to ride the bus for an hour as I did when I went to school here." She flashed a smile at Cassie and teased, "You remember Josh, don't you? He was one of the riders from the other day when we came into town."

Great, this hunk is being forced to babysit me? What if he doesn't want to be around me, or worse; what if he's the jerk of the whole school? Why hadn't she heard of this arrangement before now? This school thing could be very bad. Well, at least, I don't have to ride on a stinking bus for over an hour every morning and every night.

Her mom stopped writing on her notepad long enough to check out Cassie's mood. "You do remember Josh from yesterday, don't you? He was the boy on the horse that stopped to talk with me about his mother." She smiled. Leigh knew she had gained a few points . . . Josh was a very attractive boy, and she had seen Cassie's reaction to him.

Cassie was not able to maintain a neutral face while discussing the boys from yesterday, so she decided to change the subject. "Mom, have you noticed anything creepy about this house?" She looked at her mom's face.

Was that a flicker of unease she saw? Whatever it was, it was gone before she could be sure.

"What are you talking about, Cassie? There is nothing wrong with this beautiful home of ours. You wait until I cast my magic on this place."

At that moment, she hated her mom. Didn't she realize this was like taking a knife and twisting it in her heart? Why couldn't she see that each alteration of the house was taking her further away from the only life she had ever known? Her father, Megan and Jessica, her school, her friends--her life. They were all moving away from her. She hated it, and she hated her mother for making it all happen.

Leigh saw the look of anguish on her daughter's face and quickly changed the subject. "Cassie, would you like to go into town this afternoon? We could explore downtown Salyersville. Maybe we can get to know our new neighbors."

Cassie winced when she heard her mom say "our new neighbors" but felt a rush at the thought of leaving the farm and more importantly the house. Spending the day in the house was more than she could endure, and a hike on the farm hadn't helped. She agreed to go with her mom. She might as well find out what her life was going to be like for the next few months . . . she refused to say next three years. And besides, the alternative was to stay at the house alone, and she wasn't ready for that.

After a lunch of tuna and crackers with the remaining Fritos from their trip to the farm, the two made their way down the country road toward Salyersville. When they got close to the spot where Cassie had seen the three "hotties" the day before, she stretched herself trying to see any signs that they were close by again.

Not so lucky today. Nothing except road and fields of corn, with a couple of vegetable gardens as far as the eye could see. Leigh noticed Cassie's quick stance of alertness and smiled. Yes, she had found the key to making sure her daughter would not be miserable for long. Leigh knew that since one of the boys they had seen riding yesterday was Josh, her friend Anita's son, there was a great chance that

Josh and Cassie would become friends. Leigh was counting on it.

Hopefully, Josh could help Cassie see that life on the farm could be amazing. She would not give up the experiences and memories she had of her youth for anything.

Now was her chance to give her daughter the same gift. Cassie believed she had moved them to the farm to punish her. But Leigh wanted to offer her daughter the same wonderful life she had experienced when she was Cassie's age.

Right now, they needed to do some shopping and some business. She had to round up some business if she was going to make the farm self-sufficient. Besides, they had to have supplies and groceries. Task number one could be checked off the list after their visit into town. "Let's stop at Caudill Feed and Supply first. I need to speak with Mark, an old friend of mine."

She glanced over at her daughter, but she was engrossed in her iPod. Leigh smiled and made a left turn leading to the gravel parking lot in front of the supply store. Cassie was so involved in the music that she didn't notice the car had stopped or that they were at their destination. Leigh gave her a quick nudge and motioned her to come with her. Cassie gave a frown, unplugged, and pulled the earphones off her ears and reluctantly slid from the front seat of the Explorer.

As Cassie strolled across the gravel pavement towards the entrance of the store, she was struck with disbelief at the abundance of men with muscles and bronzed tans that paraded past her. Some nodded in her direction; some stared, and some were brave enough to greet her mom and her. Wow, so much for Salyersville having nothing to offer. Without a doubt, there's plenty of good-looking muscle-filled bodies to check out. Probably didn't do much thinking though. Bet they thought a good time was watching some old TV show like "Dukes of Hazard" or something. Cassie was beyond deluding herself into thinking that these people could understand the meaning of having a good time. What was there in this little town to allow having a good time? Then again, looking wasn't against the law and Salyersville sure had its moments for looking.

Cassie smiled as she followed her mom into the store. "Leigh Howard, you're a sight for sore eyes. How are you doing?" Cassie searched for the owner of the voice and found one of the best looking older men she had ever set her eyes on. Her mother was smiling and obviously knew this man.

Cassie's mom took on the flat dialect of the natives, "Hey, Mark, how are you?" Before the gorgeous specimen in front of them could comment her mother finished, "I've come home to stay. Grandma and Granddad left me their farm. So, Cassie and I decided to move home and get it back up and running." She pulled Cassie in front of her for Mark to see.

Mark looked at Cassie and then Leigh and let out a yelp. "Good news. Glad to see you back. I heard that since your Grandparents got sick the farm has run down."

"You're right, the farm has completely shut down, but I want to get it back to working order. That is, with a little help from you." Leigh smiled. "First, I need some workers to help clean it up and then I'll open it up to board livestock. Hopefully, it will help us make some money." She waited for a second, and before she could get a reply from Mark, she added, "What do you think? Can you help me find some good workers?"

Mark stared at Leigh, and then as if all she had said finally registered he burst out laughing. Once he got his breath back, he asked, "How many do you think you'll need, Leigh?" Cassie could tell that Mark genuinely cared for her mom. The way his eyes danced when he looked at her told a story that Cassie wasn't sure she wanted to hear. Who was this man her mom called an old friend?

Leigh seemed to be unaware of Mark's affection. She was totally into business mode. "I'd say around three or four would be enough to start. I don't have a huge amount of money, so I have to start small." She stopped long enough to offer Mark her best smile. Cassie wasn't as sure about her mother as she was about Mark, but she thought she saw a flicker of affection in her mom's eyes. They must have been very good friends from the past to exchange the looks these two were passing back and forth.

"I hear you." Mark smiled and grabbed a store notepad. "I'll work on it. Give me your phone number, and I'll give you a call once I round up a few good hands."

"Thanks, Mark. You're a good friend." Leigh smiled. "The number is the same as Granddad's; it has never changed. Do you still have it?"

"I still have the number." Mark stole an intimate look at Leigh, "Called it often back in the day." Mark caressed Leigh's shoulder and gave her a look that didn't escape Cassie. Her mom didn't show any signs of alarm or annoyance. What was this? Cassie frowned and moved closer to her mother. She was drawn to protect her mother's—What? What was she trying to protect? She felt emotions that she couldn't put a name to, but she was ready to leave. This man was too familiar with her mother.

"Mom, I thought you were taking me shopping." She inched closer to Leigh. "Can we go now?"

Leigh smiled at Mark, "Thanks, Mark. Once I get settled you'll have to come over for dinner so I can thank you."

Cassie watched while Mark smiled and again looked deep into Leigh's eyes, "Wouldn't miss it for the world. Do you cook any better than you did twenty years ago?" He and Leigh both began to laugh.

"I'll make sure it isn't Chicken Marsala. Okay?" They both laughed at their private joke, and Leigh seemed to float out of the store with Mark standing in the doorway, watching as the ladies climbed into the Explorer. A frown creased Cassie's forehead as a contented smile spread across Leigh's face.

A trip to the grocery was met with a few surprised recognitions of her mother and 'welcome homes.' Finally, they were on their way back home, hauling enough groceries for the week. Cassie couldn't believe it, but she was ready for some free time to rest and watch some television. They did get TV here in the boonies, didn't they?

After they had put away the groceries, Cassie settled in the living room to watch "Ellen." She lay down on the couch facing the old TV and soon felt sleep wash over her. She heard something about the Kardashian's and a new show plot focusing on the two younger daughters. She didn't care which Kardashians were showcased this fall; she'd rather see a rerun of anything. Cassie tried to move from the couch but found she couldn't. It was like a heavy load … a body … was sitting on top of her. She was scared. So scared. She tried to call out to her mother for help. Nothing came out of her mouth. Her bones ached as she strained against the heavy being on top of her. Something held her down refusing to give up its power over her. What or who had entered her great-grandparent's home and forced this power struggle over her.

After what seemed like an eternity, she forced her eyes open. She had to see what had trapped her … was pushing down on her. Nothing. There was nothing on top of her yet she felt the pressure. Once again, she struggled to lift her body. Without warning, the paisley pillow her mom had placed in the corner of the couch flew across the room landing on the floor. What? She was paralyzed with fear. After attempting to call her mother once again she heard her voice gasping. "Mom. Where are you? Please, Mom."

Leigh heard the fear in her daughter's voice and came running from the kitchen. "What's wrong, Cassie? Are you okay?" She could see her daughter's white ghostlike face. She ran over to the couch picking up the paisley pillow as she moved toward her daughter.

"Mom," Cassie stuttered, "That pillow just went flying across the room." Gesturing from the couch to the television, "From here to there without any reason." Tears rolled to the corners of her eyes and spilled down her checks. This was getting spooky. Cassie hated spooky.

Leigh could see the fright in Cassie's face, and heard

it in her voice. She didn't doubt Cassie's story. Her focus was on Cassie and making her feel safe. "Cassie, there has got to be an explanation. Were you sleeping?"

"Yes, but I didn't touch that pillow, believe me, I couldn't move. Mom, something was holding me down. When I began to struggle against it, the pillow went flying."

"You were dreaming, sweetie. You kicked the pillow without realizing it." Leigh stroked her daughter's head. "We'll have to watch eating tuna if it causes you to have dreams like this." Her mom giggled.

Cassie didn't giggle. Her mom's explanation didn't convince her. But what was the alternative explanation? She chose to accept her mom's rationalization. What other choice did she have? Was she to believe that something threw the pillow while lying on top of her, pressing her into the cushions of her grandma's couch? No, her mom had to be right; she had been dreaming and kicked the pillow without knowing what she was doing.

She needed to get some air. Maybe she would take a walk. This time she wouldn't go through the pasture; she would take the road that led to the adjoining farm. She called to her mom that she was going for a walk up toward the neighbor's and hurried out of the house grabbing her iPod and phone on her way out the door. Might as well check in with what was left of her Louisville life. She called Megan's phone.

"Hello." She immediately forgot the eerie happenings in the house and concentrated on her friends.

"Hello, stranger." Cassie felt relief wash over her. "It is good to hear your voice. What are you guys getting into, Megan?" She heard a shrilling scream on the other end of the phone.

"It's Cassie!" Cassie could hear the chatter in the background. She smiled. They hadn't forgotten her yet.

The phone call wasn't like being there in person, but at least she would get to hear from the gang. "Where are you, Megan? And, who's with you?" Cassie stopped on the gravel road, oblivious of her surroundings.

"We're getting blizzards from Dairy Queen. We've

decided this is going to be our place to hang this semester." Cassie listened intently, wishing she were with her friends. "Oh, Cassie, you have to hear this. Jessica and Matthew Donaldson have kind of been dating since you've been gone. I am so happy for her," Megan giggled, "and me, since all his buddies are hanging around us. We've been having some good times. We miss you, girl."

"Oh, Megan I so wish I was there with you guys. Tell everyone I miss them. Okay?"

She could hear the rush of laughter and Megan whispered, "I'll call you later?"

"Sure, okay. Have fun." Well, if she wasn't in a bad mood before, she surely was now. While she was stuck in this black hole of a town, her best friends would be enjoying wonderful times with some of the cutest boys at Male High School. How had her life become this unfair dreadful existence in Salyersville? I wonder if Damon is with them. He and Matt were good friends. She hadn't had a chance to ask Megan about him. What was the point? Wasn't like she could do anything about it from here.

She shoved her phone back into her pocket and was busy putting her ear buds in when she looked up to see a beautiful horse trotting toward her. The boy riding him looked familiar. Could it be one of the boys she had seen when her mom and she came into town? Yes, it definitely was him. She wasn't about to forget his gorgeous smile. He pulled up beside her and stopped. "Hey, pretty girl, are you lost?"

Cassie looked up at the horse and then at the perfect face looking down at her. "No . . . alas . . . just taking a walk from down the road. My mother and I are living on the Howard Farm. I'm Cassie . . . Cassie Ward. I think we met the other day on our drive to the farm." She waited while Josh nodded recognition.

"Then it's official. We're neighbors. I live on the Johnson Farm. I'm Josh Johnson. Mom said that her friend was moving back in the house and that she had a daughter; I just wasn't expecting someone as cute as you." Josh smiled. "How are you doing with the move? Was it

Cassie?"

Cassie extended her hand, "Good to meet you, Josh." She flashed him her best smile. She reached toward the horse's nose to pet him. The horse lowered his head toward her. His nose felt warm and safe. She fell in love with the horse immediately, and the owner wasn't half bad. In one swift movement, Josh slid down from the saddle and stood close to her. "This here is Wildfire. We're best friends, and it looks as if he's taking you on as his friend too."

Cassie smiled. There was that flat drawl she sometimes heard in her mother's voice. It sounded much more attractive coming from Josh.

"Thanks, Wildfire, I like you too. I'd love to be your friend."

Josh gave her a sad look, and she flashed him what she hoped was her flirty smile. "I'd like to be your friend, too, Josh." He nudged her a little, and they both laughed when Wildfire nudged them both.

They walked together in the general direction of Cassie's farm. Josh asked if the farm would start boarding livestock again. Cassie frowned at him and said, "I don't know, why? Should it be?"

He laughed. "That's what the Howard Farm has been known for my whole life. It's been strange since your granddad decided to stop keeping livestock. It's sad seeing the pasture and barns without any signs of life. Maybe now that will change since you guys have moved into the house."

"I don't know," was all Cassie could manage on the subject. She had nothing to offer. The fact was she wasn't interested in learning what her mother had planned for the farm. She just wanted to leave.

"Cassie, my friends and I are going to go four-wheeling through the hills on my farm tomorrow. Would you like to come along? You could ride behind me on my four-wheeler."

"Sure, I'd love to go." What else was she going to do all day? It could be fun. "What should I wear?" She didn't have a clue as to what four-wheeling meant.

Josh held his smile, "Wear long pants, layers of shirts so as the day gets hot you can peel them off. Bring a bag lunch with you and we'll stop for a picnic up on one of the ridges." He took a long look at Cassie and added, "We have some kind of fun when we ride."

"Sounds like fun." She said, not knowing if she completely believed it or not.

"Okay then, I'll see you around 8:00 in the morning." He swung himself back onto Wildfire and gave one last nod, and he and Wildfire were off at a run.

Cassie stared at the two as they headed back toward the Johnson Farm. They were beautiful galloping through the field and up the hill. What ... 8:00 in the morning--are you kidding me? He gets up at 8:00 just because he wants to? What is up with that? She turned back toward her house and for the first time since she had been there; she had something to look forward to doing.

She stopped in her tracks; she had totally forgotten her friends back home having fun without her. She'd just have to find some fun for herself tomorrow. She picked up her pace not noticing the grin plastered all over her face. Hopefully, she would enjoy Josh and his friends and four-wheeling.

She made her way over the hill and as she started to descend she could see the roof of Grandma and Granddad's house. It should have been welcoming, yet she felt that all too familiar dread. She slowed her pace and tried to get a grip on her emotions before going inside.

FIVE

True to his word, Josh knocked on Cassie's door at 8:00 o'clock the next morning. Cassie found it easy to get up early because she was excited about the day. She was ready and waiting when Josh arrived. Leigh was puzzled. Cassie always had a hard time getting started in the mornings. Yet, there she was bright eyed and ready. She saw the excitement in Cassie's mood as her daughter bounced around the house getting ready.

Giggling, Leigh made her way to the front door. She hoped Cassie would find some good friends today. "Good morning, Josh. Need some hot coffee to get you started this morning?"

Josh stepped into the living room then allowed his eyes to search the room for his date. "No, thank you. I've already had my cup this morning." He flashed his handsome smile down at Leigh. He noted that Cassie's mom was just an older version of Cassie. She had the same blue eyes and blond hair. They were both tall enough but not too tall…he'd guess around 5'6"--and if the mom's body were any indication, Cassie wouldn't be losing her knockout shape as she grew older. He willed his mind to focus on the conversation. "Drink one first thing before going to the barn every morning." He stepped past Leigh finding his way to Cassie's side and gave her a huge smile. "Are you ready for a day of four-wheeling?"

She smiled back, "Yes, I'm excited. I've never gone four-wheeling, but it sounds like fun. I must admit I'm a bit nervous about climbing these mountains."

"Don't worry; I go every Saturday and Sunday. Haven't gotten hurt or had any bad luck yet. I'm very careful. You have to know when to let the mountain win." Leigh noticed his quick smile when he looked at her daughter. She was happy for the developing friendship, although she didn't know a lot about her friend's son or what Anita would think about this budding friendship. She imagined Anita's face if their two children ended up more than friends. Just thinking of Anita's reaction made her want to laugh. She decided to dismiss the direction of her thoughts before she got carried away. After all, Cassie and Josh had only met yesterday.

"You two be careful and be home by six, okay? I'll worry if it begins to get dark and you are out in the woods." Leigh looked at Cassie and then at Josh.

Josh answered, "Sure thing, Mrs. Ward. I'll make sure we make it back to the farm before six." He turned his attention to Cassie. "Are you ready City Girl? Let's make you into a mountain climbing country girl." Leigh and Josh both laughed.

Cassie frowned at him, "That is just not going to happen. I'll always be a city girl at heart."

"Talk to me six months from now." He grinned at her. Leigh didn't know which was surer that they were the correct one in this argument, Cassie or Josh.

Cassie hugged her mom goodbye and felt a tug from her heart. She didn't want to leave her mom alone in the house all day. She felt more than a little anxious about the events that had occurred in the house but her mom didn't seem to mind. Maybe nothing creepy had happened to her. Maybe Cassie was allowing her imagination to run wild. This was her great-grandparents' home. Great-grandparents that she loved and they had loved her. As much as she didn't want her mom left alone all day, she was relieved for a day away from the house.

She bounced out the front door behind Josh, ready to climb on the back of the huge black and gold Honda four-wheeler. Josh started the engine and away they went toward Josh's farm. Cassie waved at her mom and she waved back. To her surprise, her mom didn't look lonely or forlorn. She looked happy—but who was that standing next to her mother? Had one of her mom's old friends come to welcome her back to the neighborhood? She looked a bit dramatic, like she was dressed for a costume party. Her white, flowing dress was straight out of the early 1900s.

Even if her mother's friends dressed on the weird side, she was relieved that her mom would have company to keep her occupied this Saturday.

Forgetting about her mom and her friend, Cassie focused on the wind hitting her face and the pull of the four-wheeler as they made their way up a steep hill. She closed her eyes. Watching the four-wheeler climb up the small trail leading up the mountain was more than she could handle. Rocks and dirt made the vehicle pull, spin, and spit, as it moved up the hill. Cassie was relieved when Josh told her to hang on tight and that is exactly what she did. His body felt good and strong. She could feel his muscles strain as he pushed and teased the engine up the hill. Once they were on top, she kept her arms around his waist but didn't grip as tightly as before. So far this was fun. Didn't he say there were others that would be joining them? Where were they?

As if Josh had read her mind, he turned to face her and announced they would be meeting the others across the ridge and down on the Howard farm near the stream. Were they going back around to the stream she had visited yesterday? She hoped not, she'd had enough of that place for a while. Yet, that is exactly where she found herself as Josh brought the four-wheeler to a stop. The goose bumps were back. You'd think she was a baby from the way she was acting—afraid of the "boogieman." She laughed nervously at her own conversation with herself.

Josh got off the four-wheeler and announced they would stay there until the rest of the gang made it. He helped Cassie roll off the back of the four-wheeler and then spread out a blanket near the stream. Cassie felt the hair on her arms rise when she saw he had put the blanket next to the huge tree. To Cassie's dismay it was the same spot she had visited yesterday. She felt herself holding her breath with the fear of what might happen next. Please hurry and get here so we can be on our way.

Josh motioned Cassie to sit down. She found her way over to the blanket and slipped down beside him. She sat rigid, not knowing what might happen. She remembered yesterday's events and could not relax. Josh misunderstood why she was so preoccupied and laughed, "You look so worried. I'm not going to bite you, I promise. Let's get to know each other. If we're going to be neighbors, we might as well learn about each other." He waited but didn't get any response from Cassie. "Okay, I'll go first. I'm sixteen, almost seventeen, and go to Salyersville High." He turned toward Cassie, "Are you going to go there too?"

Cassie made herself focus on Josh while she desperately tried to dismiss the feeling of anxiousness. "That is what my mom told me yesterday. I hadn't really thought about what I was going to do for school. I dread riding the bus every day. I've never had to ride a school bus. Back home I walked up the street to St. Mary's." Cassie looked down. "I really want to go home and spend my sophomore year with all my friends, but my mom is determined to make us live here. Only problem with her plan is that I'm just as determined to go back home."

"So, who is winning this struggle?" Josh looked at Cassie. What he saw was a girl torn with anguish but what he didn't realize was that the look was more about where they were sitting than the tug of wills between Cassie and her mother.

"She's winning," Cassie mumbled. "But she will come to her senses once she gets over her head with the farm business." Cassie flashed a smile. She realized that Josh might not be on her side in this battle with her mom.

"And if she doesn't give in?" He had a serious look on his face. It was a genuine question. She couldn't believe she had brought their joyful fun day down to this serious discussion. She decided to change the mood for the better.

"I'll be your neighbor for a very long time." She gave him a flirtatious smile. She was beginning to like this boy.

"I can think of worse things." Josh declared.

Was he flirting with her? If he was flirting, she liked it. "I guess I can think of worse things too." At this moment, Cassie was feeling very close to this boy that she had only just met.

"Thanks, Josh, for inviting me on this ride. I hope you're having as good of a time as I am." She declared.

Josh leaned close to Cassie, "I'm having a great time. It's worth it just to watch you as we start up the hills. I must admit, I have enjoyed this time with you very much." They looked at each other a little longer than necessary. Just as Cassie was beginning to feel self-conscious they heard the roar of the other four-wheelers. Relief flowed over her body. She saw four four-wheelers coming over the hill. Three of them had two people on board. The fourth had a solo rider—one very good-looking boy who looked familiar. He was one of the boys she had seen that first day on their way to the farm. Seth was his name. No way was she going to forget that. This day was getting better by the minute.

Josh stood and led Cassie over to the other four-wheelers. "Guys, this is Cassie. She and her mom moved to the Howard farm. Actually, the Howard's were her great-grandparents." Cassie smiled and waved at the group. They all greeted her. Cassie felt a genuine welcome from the group of riders. Her spirit soared.

"Ready to ride? Let's do it." Josh yelled as he straddled his four-wheeler. Hopping on the back, Cassie pulled her arms around Josh's waist. If felt right. No one seemed to notice the closeness the two had developed so quickly. The roar of the engines broke the silence of the woods, and off they went, going for the top of the mountain. Again, Cassie felt her heart pound with fear and excitement of the danger that lurked at the wheels of the monster they were riding. She felt protected by Josh. She squeezed closer to Josh's back and smiled as she closed her eyes.

Later, the group stopped for lunch. There were five boys and four girls, and they all laughed and kidded while stealing each other's sandwiches and snacks. Cassie hadn't laughed so much since before her mom and dad divorced. Throughout lunch, she noticed Josh glancing at her, and she couldn't help but look back. They smiled, and it felt comfortable. Cassie felt like a girl with friends, good friends. These friends were nothing like what she imagined. Maybe living here wouldn't be so bad.

Slowly she began learning everyone's name. Jake and Seth she already knew from the encounter on her first day in town. She met Sarah, Jake's four-wheeler partner. She liked Sarah immediately. She was open and chatty, and she made Cassie feel welcome, as though she had been part of the group from the beginning.

Will was with Lindsey. They seemed close, and Cassie guessed they were more than just riding partners. By the end of the day, she had met Cameron and his partner, Carol Ann. They were the quiet ones of the group.

Usually when this many people came together, there'd be at least one that was an instigator of trouble, but Cassie was finding it hard to find that person in this group. These were going to be her friends. Life was sweet.

After a wonderful afternoon of riding and meeting new friends the day was coming to an end. Josh split away from the group and started down the path toward Cassie's farm. Everyone called their goodbyes over the roar of the engines. Each promised to do it again next week. Cassie could feel the wind hit her smiling face. This had been the best day she could remember in a long time. She settled in behind Josh and relaxed.

Josh pulled the vehicle up to her front door. Cassie didn't want the day to end. She invited Josh in, but he declined. "I have chores to do before it gets dark. But, thanks and I'd love to come over tomorrow just to hang out." He smiled down at Cassie as she pretended to think about the proposal for a moment, then with a sly look agreed to hang out with Josh at the farm the next day.

"Thanks for a wonderful day, Josh. I had the best time. I hope everyone was okay with me tagging along." She looked deep into his eyes as if trying to detect truth in them.

Josh laughed, "Are you kidding?" He looked at her face, "You are one of us now, girl. It's your duty to tag along now that you are a part of the Lick Creek crowd."

Cassie smiled and rolled Lick Creek over her tongue.

Who would have thought anything good could have happened to her from Lick Creek? She had enjoyed being a part of the crew today. She looked up at Josh and whispered, "See you tomorrow, Lick Creek friend." They both laughed one last time, and then Josh turned the four-wheeler and headed home.

Cassie made her way into the house. She expected to see her mom, but the house was quiet. The goose bumps were creeping up on her once again. What is it with this house? She called out to her mom, but the silence was heavy. She mustered enough courage to explore downstairs but found nothing. The stairs creaked as she made her way to the second floor; her heart pounding so hard that she could swear her sweatshirt was bouncing. "Mom, are you up here?" No answer. The last thing she wanted to do right now was walk through this house with all the lights off. She turned lights on in each room as she walked through. In her bedroom, she heard a faint pounding coming from the back of the room. Just as she was ready to run from the room she saw her mom's head raise above a stack of boxes in the corner.

Leigh saw her daughter. "Hi honey. How was your day?"

"Sorry about the mess. I'm trying to find our kitchen stuff. I promise to clean my mess up before I quit. How was it?" Obviously, her mom had plunged into another one of her projects. Cassie could remember time after time when her mom would throw herself into a project while Cassie and her dad laughed at her passion for whatever it happened to be that month. Here she was doing it again. Good for her, it would keep her happy … for a while.

Cassie smiled. "New project?"

"Maybe, little girl, maybe. Well…how was your day?"

"Great! Four-wheeling is so much fun. I met a lot of kids from the Creek, and I think they liked me. Josh was great." She couldn't keep the smile from showing through as she spoke.

Leigh was smiling too, happy to see her daughter in a better mood. "That is just great, Cassie. Do you know any of their families? I bet I know their family, especially if they are from around this area."

"No, Mom, I didn't take resumes. I only got first names, but they all live close." She giggled and then became serious. "Oh, by the way, is it okay for Josh to come over tomorrow just to hang out?"

"HANG OUT?" It was Leigh's turn to giggle. "I haven't heard that term in a long time. It sounds funny coming from you."

"That's what Josh said, so I'm guessing that's what people do around here … 'Hang Out'."

"Sure, Josh may come over tomorrow to 'Hang Out'."

"Thanks, I'll tell him to come on over to 'Hang Out'." They both laughed. It had been a while since they had laughed and felt this comfortable with each other. If felt right. It felt natural.

"So, how was your day? Did you have fun with your company?"

Leigh looked at Cassie; "I didn't see a soul all day. Just me and my project. You know how I get, can't focus on anything but the task at hand. But, Cassie, I love this one. I can really see a difference with each change I make."

"Mom, who was the lady standing on the porch with you this morning as Josh and I left? I just assumed that it was one of your high school friends come for a visit."

"Honey, there hasn't been anyone at the house today except for me. Believe me, I would have known if I'd had a visitor. Why would you think someone came to visit?"

Cassie could feel the skin on her neck begin to crawl. "Mom, I saw a woman standing next to you when I waved bye to you this morning. Are you trying to tell me there wasn't anyone on the porch with you this morning?"

Leigh stared at her daughter, "Cassie, no one has been to this house today."

"I saw her standing beside of you as you waved bye to Josh and me." Cassie struggled to keep her voice from shaking. "She was wearing a white dress that looked like it was soft and it flowed with the wind. I even made the comment that she was a little overdressed for a morning visit." Cassie began to pace around the room. She could not process the information. It didn't make sense. If anyone except her mother was saying this she wouldn't believe it, but her mom wouldn't tell anything but the truth.

"Could you see her face?" asked Leigh. She was sure her daughter felt she had seen someone standing on the porch. Leigh would have to ask the right questions to find out what made Cassie think someone was on the porch. "Was she next to the porch post?" Maybe the new furniture covers caused her to see what wasn't there. Cassie's face told her mother that she saw what she saw, and she would not believe otherwise. Leigh decided to let it go. "I'm not sure what happened, Cassie, but no one came to the house today."

Cassie looked as white as a ghost. She was trembling and pacing up and down in front of the fireplace. Leigh could see she was terribly upset. "Honey, calm down. I'm sure there is a perfectly good explanation. Please don't allow this to ruin your good day."

Cassie heard the truth in her mother's words and tried to breath. "Mom, have you noticed anything eerie about this house?" Her eyes were piercing her mother's trying to find an answer to what was happening with her and her great-grandparents' house.

Cassie saw a flicker in her mom's eyes. Leigh recovered quickly and replied, "It's just a house, Cassie. Grandma and Granddad wanted us to have it, to enjoy it. They would never cause us any harm."

Cassie looked away from her mom. Leigh was dancing around the question. Something odd had happened with her mom. This wasn't any comfort—only confirmation of what she had been afraid to acknowledge, that it wasn't just her imagination. Now she had to climb those stairs and sleep in that bed, not knowing what was watching her. "I guess I need to go to bed." Cassie's face had no color. She looked as if she was ready to run screaming from the house.

Leigh looked at her daughter and asked, "I have

unloaded a lot of stuff in your room, how about sleeping with me? It will just be until I get all of the mess cleaned up?" Relieved, Cassie smiled and nodded yes.

The next morning, Cassie woke up in the large four-poster bed all by herself. She rolled over to see the sun shining in the window. It was going to be a good day. Josh was coming over. He was her first real friend in Salyersville. She pushed the events with the house away from her thoughts and climbed out of bed.

Now to brave the upstairs so she could get her clothes and take a shower. As she stepped into the room, she was amazed that she didn't feel the usual prickly feeling. The room was sunny and pleasant—if you just looked at the surface. She sauntered over to the closet that stored all her worldly possessions and removed a black polka dot shirt and her best blue jeans. She laughed at herself. She was trying to look good for someone she had met only two days ago. But her instinct told her that she and Josh were going to be good friends … maybe more … but if not, she needed some good friends, and he was the cutest best friend she could find. Once she was ready, she ran down the stairs and found her mom working on the decorating again.

Leigh looked up and nodded her approval of Cassie's clothing choices and kept on painting the living room wall. Great, Josh would have to smell fresh paint the whole time he visited. How embarrassing. "Mom, did you have to start painting when you know Josh is coming over?"

Leigh stopped in mid-stroke of the paint roller. "Surely, you two won't stay cooped up in this house all day." She finished her stroke and stepped back to admire her choice of paint color. The new color made the living room feel like home.

"Well, I don't know where we might end up, but it would have been nice to have the option of hanging out around the television."

"Why don't you guys go over to Uncle Ray's and check on the horse he has asked us to board?" Leigh rolled her paintbrush in the paint. "That would give you something to do and be helpful at the same time." Leigh made another long stroke down the wall. Cassie studied her mother. What was the deal? Why was she trying to get them out of the house?

"What's going on, Mom?" Cassie looked suspiciously at her mother. "Why do you want Josh and me to leave?"

"No reason, just making a suggestion."

Leigh finished the wall and turned to face her daughter. "Alright." Leigh paused, struggling with her inner self, "Mark called and wants to meet with me to finalize a deal for the farm, and I'd like to invite him over to discuss the details."

Cassie's face fell like a rock. Her mom's frown was only seconds behind. It was obvious Leigh was wondering how long it was going to take her daughter to accept their new life. The divorce had been tough. Cassie knew that when her dad remarried it was devastating. Why hadn't she and her mom been enough? That realization had killed something deep in her mother's core, and it had forever changed Cassie.

If Dad had thought about anyone but himself, he'd have realized how much he was hurting his family. Now, they both had to move on with their lives. Life could be okay here ... Mom had loved living here when she was my age. She hoped that time would heal.

Six

While both mother and daughter stood with long sad faces, there was a knock on the door. Cassie opened the door to greet Josh. "Hey, Josh. Please come in, sorry for the odor. My mom decided that today would be a good day to start painting our living room." She shot Leigh one of her "I could kill you" glances.

Leigh winced and looked to Josh. "How is your mom, Josh?" Without waiting for him to answer she added, "I need to go visit her. It has just been so busy since we arrived."

Josh came closer to the large tray of paint and responded, "She'd love that. She was complaining this morning about being stuck at the farm and can't get over to see you." Josh looked at Cassie and then at Leigh. It was obvious that something was going on, and he had stepped in the middle. "Cassie, want to go into town? The guys you met yesterday are going bowling, and we could join them if you'd like. Do you bowl?" Josh grinned, "Or, a better question, are you any good at bowling?"

Cassie snapped out of her mood and handed back, "Are you good enough to be seen playing with this pro?" She flashed Josh a smile.

Josh looked at her and asked, "Leigh, is she as good as she pretends?"

Leigh looked at her daughter and said, "She and her dad use to be partners on a bowling team." She smiled at Cassie. "They won the Old Louisville Bowling championship last year."

Josh gave Cassie a surprised look. "Wow, glad to have that bit of information. It'll come in handy when the others start bragging." He grabbed Cassie's hand and said, "Let's go champ; we have work to do." They laughed and bid Leigh goodbye as they bounced out the door.

Leigh smiled, hoping Cassie would forget her bad mood while she was out with her friends. She began painting again. The silence was deafening, so she turned on the television just to have some noise while she worked. As she walked back to the painting tray and bent down to pick up her brush, the television went off. It wasn't the electricity because the lights were working. She walked back over and turned it on again. As she picked up the paint roller, the television went off again. Was the switch going bad? She didn't have the money to replace the thing. She turned the set on again and waited. After a few minutes she decided that it was working fine. Then, without warning, it went off again. Exasperated, she decided to leave it alone. As soon as she resumed her painting, the television came on. "What the...." This was getting weird. As she turned toward the cantankerous television she heard the front door.

Standing in the doorway was Mark; at least an hour early. "Mark, I wasn't expecting you this soon." Leigh quickly gained her composure and offered, "Come on in, please."

"I'm sorry, Leigh. I know I'm early, but I thought I'd stop and ask if you'd like to go for a ride into town. We could stop at Betty's and have a piece of ice cream cake." He searched her face. "What do you think? Just like old times, we could hang out and catch up."

Leigh thought about the television and decided this would be a great relief. "I'd love to go. With my TV going on and off on its own, I think that a few hours away from it is the break I need. Let's go have some cake." She stored her paint behind the couch and closed the door.

She climbed into Mark's pickup, and time melted away. She looked at Mark as he slid into the driver's seat. "Just like old times."

Mark gave her hand a squeeze and declared, "Good times."

"It's been a long time since I've been in your truck, headed to town," Leigh said. "Remember your old truck, the one that sounded as if a freight train was coming up the road? Every time you came to pick me up my Mother would wince." They both laughed.

"Yeah, your dad would make sure he was working in the front yard so that he could give me the evil eye." Mark looked at Leigh and held her eyes for a moment, "To tell you the truth; it worked." He pulled his eyes back to the highway; "It sure kept me honest with you. I mean if he cared that much for you and I cared that much for you than I had to be sincere and true about our relationship. Leigh, you always had my true devotion." He took a long look at her. "We were happy, weren't we, Leigh?"

"Yes, we were happy." He reached over and gently held her hand and Leigh gave his a light squeeze. As they rode together, she looked out the window. Memories came flooding back. Time had passed; she was no longer that young girl in love with a handsome boy. She was a grown woman and a single mom with a teenage daughter that didn't want her mother to have a love life.

She didn't want Cassie to hate Mark, and she wasn't sure how to prevent that from happening. Cassie was determined to hate everything and everyone Leigh knew from Lick Creek. Mark didn't stand a chance. She dropped Mark's hand and turned so she could look at him.

"Mark, I have just gotten back home and I have a huge job to do if I plan on making Granddad's farm provide for Cassie and me. I want to make this work. I love living here. I have to make Cassie love it too. I have to give it my best shot." She looked at Mark with pleading eyes. He smiled and placed his hand on her cheek.

"I understand what you are saying, little girl. I will be on my best behavior and wait until you think it's time for us to see each other on a friendlier basis. Right now, I'm just an old friend helping out an old friend by getting her farm up and running. That sound alright, Mrs. Ward?"

Leigh smiled, "Please call me Leigh, Mr. Caudill." She stared at his face. They had been so close once. How had she let it slip away? But, maybe if she had stayed, Mark would have been just like Jack. Time seemed to change and destroy the way things are in the beginning. But, today she was back home and Mark was driving her into town. She was going to enjoy every second of this day.

"Let's stop at the Frozen Corner for some homemade peach ice cream before we head home, what do you think? Do they still have it anymore? Please tell me they still make the best peach ice cream in the world." She didn't wait for Mark to respond. "When we decided to move back, one of the first things I looked forward to was the peach ice cream at the Frozen Corner."

"Sure, once we talk with Jim and Ted, we'll stop for a visit at the Frozen Corner." Mark mused, "I bet Nancy would love to see you since you were one of her best customers." He laughed.

"Okay, so I loved the ice cream; you didn't turn any of it down as I recall." Mark's smile spread across his entire face.

"It is good to have you home, Mrs. Ward. Stopping at the Frozen Corner has officially become a priority on our to-do list."

They settled into a long-ago comfort and rode in silence. As they came closer to the Smith farm, Mark looked over at Leigh, "Are you ready to get started?"

"Let's do it. Thank you, Mark; thank you for all you are doing for Cassie and me."

"Wouldn't have it any other way. There it is—the Smith Farm."

Seven

Cassie and Josh arrived at Joseph's Bowling alley just in time to see Sarah and Jake, two of the people Cassie had ridden with yesterday, walk in the alley. "Looks like we're just in time for the fun. Let's go win some free food, what do you say?" Josh grabbed Cassie's hand and pulled her into the alley.

"Free food, that's what you are playing for, free food? Here I think we are on this mission to rack up some major cash, and I find out it is for free food?" Cassie snickered.

Josh couldn't help but laugh at Cassie's description of the group's ongoing challenge. "Yelp, free food if we win; we pay if we lose." Josh mocked seriousness, "Jake can eat a lot of pizzas … just saying."

Cassie pulled her serious face, "Oh, I got your back. There will be no food for us to buy today."

"Now that's what I'm talking about." Josh escorted her to the counter for their shoes.

While waiting on their bowling shoes, Sarah spied her two friends. "Josh, Cassie, we're over here." She squealed. "Come over to lane three when you guys get finished." She bounced away looking for Jake.

"Are they a couple?" Cassie asked.

"They've been a couple ever since seventh grade," Josh replied. "True love…I guess it never dies."

"I wouldn't be too sure about that," Cassie snapped. "Just look at all the divorced people that are living broken lives just because they allowed love to die."

Josh saw the hurt and anger in Cassie's face and decided to change the subject. "Ready to go kick some Lick Creek butt?"

"Let's do it, partner," she grabbed Josh's outstretched hand, and off they went to lane three. Cassie saw the same crowd she had ridden with yesterday. She already felt comfortable with the group after spending the day with them yesterday. They had all made her feel as if she had been one of them since the moment they had driven up on their four-wheelers. She noticed that there was one girl that she didn't remember from yesterday's ride. She had long black shiny hair—pretty, but something wasn't right with her attitude. She looked at everyone as if she didn't want to be seen with them. Like she was too good for them. If she's unhappy to be with these people, then why is she here? Cassie thought.

Sarah pulled Cassie over and introduced the two girls, "Kari this is Cassie, she just moved on to the Howard farm. Cassie this is Kari one of the crew from Lick Creek." Sarah hesitated, "Kari lives down on the main drag. Her parents are Cottrell's Dentistry, so if you have a toothache you know who to call."

Cassie nodded toward Kari and got a sniff in return. Not knowing how to react, she watched as Kari rudely scrutinized her in front of everyone. Obviously uncomfortable with the examination, Cassie searched for Josh, willing him to come to her rescue. Josh did not fail her.

He stepped up beside Cassie and actually laid his arm around her shoulder, casually, as if he had done it often. Cassie wasn't sure which was causing her body heat to rise, this rude person piercing her with her eyes or Josh being so comfortable with her. She liked it more than she wanted to admit. She knew her face was flushed and hated that her new friends would see it.

Thank goodness for Sarah. As the tension grew, Sarah rescued her by bringing everyone's attention to the bowling balls. "I claim the red ball; want to share, Cassie?" Sarah winked at Cassie, "Only my new best friend is allowed to share the luck."

Cassie flashed Sarah a look of relief and mumbled, "Sure," without even trying out the ball. She could care less which ball fit best. The only thing that had resonated from the encounter was that Sarah had declared her as her new best friend. Life in Salyersville might not be so bad after all, even with Miss Snob Kari.

Once the game was underway, Sarah asked Cassie to help her with buying the drinks. When they were alone, she leaned over to Cassie and whispered, "Don't let Kari get under your skin. She is just jealous of Josh." Sarah paused to check Cassie's reaction and then continued, "She is totally in love with him, but Josh won't have anything to do with her." Sarah paused again, then declared, "She had her chance, and she blew it."

Cassie heard more than Sarah had wanted to tell. "Did Josh and Kari date?" She looked at Sarah and saw her squirm.

"Okay, might as well know the sordid details up front." She frowned and reluctantly gave in, "Yes, they dated."

"For how long?" Cassie asked not allowing Sarah to escape her unrelenting stare. Sarah had no choice other than spill the whole story.

Sarah pulled in a long labored breath, "Okay, a little over a year, I think. Josh was miserable but would not break it off with her. No one knows why he stayed with her so long; it was obvious he wasn't into her." She took a moment to search Cassie's face. "We all wanted him to break it off and get a life." She shook her head. "Josh was so miserable but wouldn't talk with any of us about what was going on with them. Finally, Kari got bored and had a temper tantrum that ended with a breakup."

Sarah again checked Cassie's reaction and cautiously continued. "She had no idea that if Josh got away for a while, he'd have the good sense not to jump back into the relationship. She has tried everything to get him back, but Josh just isn't biting." Sarah was relieved that Cassie was still listening and interested. "Now, in her twisted mind, you are the reason Josh has lost interest." Sarah smiled apologetically, and Cassie couldn't help but laugh out loud and give her a great big hug. Sarah sighed with relief.

"I am soooo glad you aren't taking this all wrong,

Cassie. You know, I've seen Josh having more fun these past two days than I saw him have the whole year he was with Kari."

"Well, good, but Josh and I are just good friends. I hope I can be there for him if he needs someone to help him see her the way everyone else does."

Sarah smiled, "Just friends, eh? Of course, you are JUST friends." This time it was Sarah's laugh that filled the bowling alley.

True to Cassie's promise, she was a force to be reckoned with; she and Josh won every game. Josh's face beamed. "My secret weapon. So glad I could pull her away from the big city to help a friend out." Josh put his arm around Cassie and pulled her close for all their friends to see. "Cassie, what are you feeling for food tonight?"

Their friends were all grumbling in good fun, but they just liked the challenge Cassie brought to the game. Seth told Cameron they'd have to sneak down to the bowling alley this week to practice for next week's payback. Everyone left the alley laughing except Kari. She had something more significant going on and didn't have time for such juvenile things. Cassie could have sworn she had heard someone whisper, "Good riddance." Sounded like there was a consensus that Kari was not the popular friend they all loved. For some unknown reason, this made Cassie feel sorry for her.

After stopping at the local pizza place with their friends paying the bill, Cassie and Josh headed back to Lick Creek road. Josh needed to get home to do his chores. The closer they got to home the more the old feelings of dread, anger, and hurt crept back into her mind. Cassie didn't want Josh to see this side of her, so she talked without stopping. When they finally made it to Cassie's house, Josh pulled his truck to the side of the road, stopped, leaned over and before Cassie knew what was going on, she felt Josh's soft lips caressing her own. It was gentle and new and knowing and lovely. She was falling fast and hard, but what if he did this with all the girls around here?

She pulled away and mumbled, "Do you welcome

every new neighbor this way, neighbor boy?"

Josh looked at her for what seemed like a very long time and then leaned in to kiss her again. A long lingering kiss that was soft yet consumed her. Wow. Country boys could beat city boys in the kissing department any day—at least this country boy could.

This time he was the one to pull away. Cassie was too weak to react at all. She would have stayed there without leaving. Josh looked down at her and breathed, "I'll see you tomorrow."

"What are we doing tomorrow?" Cassie asked, trying to clear her head.

Josh pulled himself up and laughed loud. "We can't play all the time, Miss Ward." He leaned in close to Cassie; "We are enrolling you in Salyersville High."

"Oh," Cassie wrinkled her nose. "I forgot." Her face became serious. "How is that going to be Josh? What is school like here?"

"I imagine it is the same as other places; classes, teachers, friends, lunch, lockers; you know, school." Josh gave her a comforting squeeze, "The teachers overall are good." He watched Cassie fight with herself, trying to make the newness okay. "I'll help you get signed up for the good ones tomorrow morning."

Cassie paused for a moment and then looked into his eyes, "Thank you, Josh." She looked past him out his window and then back to his eyes, "You have made this difficult week a very enjoyable one. I am not going to worry about school since you'll be there."

She noticed that Josh had not offered for her to ride to school with him. Cassie knew his mother had promised he would drive her but she wanted Josh to ask her himself. Maybe he didn't want to ride to school with her. Maybe he had other things to do in the mornings other than driving her around. She would rather ride the bus then have Josh forced to drive her. She smiled. "How bad is the bus ride?"

Josh took a hard look at her and declared, "You are going to ride with me." He was almost angry. "Why would you think I'd drive by you while you wait for a bus?"

Cassie smiled again. It was getting to be a habit, this smiling thing. "What time should I expect you?"

"We can leave Lick Creek around seven and make it in plenty of time." Josh flashed his irresistible smile at Cassie and chuckled, "See you tomorrow around seven?"

"You got it, farmer boy." She gave him her most flirty look and pronounced, "Now, go forth and feed animals." They laughed and parted ways.

As Cassie walked toward the house, she could feel the tension in her body rise. She put the feeling behind her and entered what was now her home. Although she wanted to see how her mom's day had gone—they had not parted on good terms. It was time to face the music. As she walked through the living room into the dining room, she couldn't help but notice the impressive changes to each room. Her mom had been busy. The house was taking on a more modern feel and yet, she had retained the touch of her Grandmother's decor. Leigh had a knack for decorating.

Cassie walked into the kitchen … Grandma's kitchen. Her mom was not a cook, so the kitchen would be the last room to get a makeover. Leigh was standing in front of the stove making tea. "Hey honey, want to have some tea with me?"

"I'll take a cup." She searched her mom's face trying to assess the damage. "Well, how was your day?" Cassie plunged ahead, might as well get it over with, no need to dance around the elephant in the room.

Leigh looked at her daughter. Then she burst out, "We have horses and cows that are coming to be housed at Howard Farm." She screamed like a young teenager. "And, I have two hired hands that will start tomorrow walking the fence to make sure the farm is ready for the livestock. It is happening, Cassie."

Cassie watched her mother. She had not been this happy for a long time. The joy had been gone ever since her father had walked out on them. Cassie realized for the first time the affect this year had on her mother. She had been a selfish teenager, and her mother had been so supporting and patient with her. Maybe this move was exactly what they both needed. They had only been here a short time, and they both were happy. She smiled at her mom and held up her teacup and declared, "Here's to the Howard Farm and the Ward women that are destined to make it happen."

Her mother raised her cup and announced, "Here, here."

As they drank their toast, there was a loud noise that came from upstairs. It was so loud that both Leigh and Cassie jumped. They looked at each other with their eyes wide. Cassie felt the tension come back into her body. "Mom, what was that?"

Leigh quickly regained her composure and calmly stated, "It must have been those boxes I have been sorting through."

Just as Cassie was agreeing with her mother, a hollow, ringing sound reverberated through the house. It was like someone had pounded a hammer on the brick of the fireplace. Again they both jumped. "Mom, there is something happening with this house." Cassie was desperate. "I keep experiencing things."

Leigh was shocked at the panic she saw wash over her daughter. Cassie had never been afraid of the dark or of monsters. This reaction was out of character. "What kind of things, Cassie?" Her mom quizzed.

Cassie fought to keep her composure. "Things, like the woman with you yesterday."

"Cassie, the lady you saw must have been the furniture cushions making an impression of a woman." Leigh waved a dismissive hand at Cassie's suggestion. "This is your Grandma and Granddad's home." She looked into Cassie's tear stained face. "They wanted us to live here. This was their wish. There is nothing wrong with this house."

Cassie stared at her mother. She was calm and she wasn't afraid. "You're right, mom. Granddad and Grandma would want us to be happy here." Wasn't it better to agree with her mother than give in to her fears?

Leigh, ready to dismiss the incident asked, "Ready for bed? We both have a big day tomorrow." Leigh yawned and stretched.

Cassie's face was evidence that she was still upset. Leigh's heart broke for her daughter. "Honey, you want to sleep in that big old bed of Grandma's and Granddad's?" Cassie was grateful for her mother's willingness to give her time to adjust.

Cassie quickly agreed to sleep in her mom's bed. She raced up the stairs to grab her pajamas, only stopping long enough to check the boxes. She wasn't surprised when she found them, still neatly stacked in the closet. Each box rested where it had been carefully placed the night before. Nothing was out of place.

What was it with this house?

Eight

Cassie raced to be ready for her first day of school. She was not only starting in a new school with all new people, but this was her sophomore year. Josh was a junior as were most of the kids she had met. However, Carol Ann and Sarah were both in her sophomore class. She hoped she would get to see them as she went through her classes today. She had taken special effort to look nice. Of course, it had nothing to do with a boy named Josh taking her to school.

Once she was ready, she walked downstairs to find her mother with an egg sandwich and orange juice. She took a few bites and drank her juice knowing her mother would not allow her to leave without eating something. Her mother's philosophy was that everyone needed to have breakfast. She had learned early; eat without arguing. "You look NICE." Her mom exclaimed. "Looking forward to the new school?"

"Not exactly," Cassie frowned. "I'd rather be going to my old school; the school with all my friends that I have known my whole life."

Leigh proclaimed, "Your new friends will be there, and I am predicting you will have a wonderful sophomore year."

Cassie opened her mouth to protest when the knock came. She opened the door to find Josh, looking as handsome as always with his bright smile. "Hey, girl, are you ready?" Looking at his invisible watch, "You don't want to be late on your first day." He laughed at his own joke, not waiting to see if anyone else thought this was as funny as he did. That was one of the things Cassie was learning to like about Josh. His ability to be his honest self, he was who he was … period. Cassie laughed not at the joke so much as at the boy telling the joke!

"Let's go" She shouted. They bound from the house and raced to Josh's Chevy pickup. Cassie climbed in the passenger side and waited for Josh who wasted no time in starting the truck and driving away.

Leigh watched the two as they turned onto the road. She knew that Josh would make sure Cassie had a good day on her first day at Salyersville High. She turned to go back into the house when she noticed someone walking through her living room. It was a woman. She stood with her back to Leigh, next to the fireplace. How did anyone get past her while she was on the porch? It must be Anita, coming in by the kitchen. She was so glad her old friend had come for a visit.

She shouted from the porch, "Anita, I'm so glad you came over. Did you see the kids...?" Her voice trailed off when she got close to the fireplace; the woman had disappeared. No one was there. She searched in each room, but there was no sign of her friend. Puzzled, Leigh decided she'd call Anita to apologize. She must have thought Leigh was gone and left through the kitchen door. Leigh knew she would hear from Anita for leaving her back door open. She went to lock it, but it was already locked.

Leigh's hands shook just for a moment and then she reasoned that Anita must have locked the door on her way out. She'd call Anita to apologize. As she walked through the house, she remembered Cassie's insistence that she had seen a woman on the front porch. She pushed the eerie feeling from her thoughts and grabbed her cell phone. She walked outside on the front porch and sat on the refurbished swing. She was so proud of the porch furniture.

"Anita, hi, it's Leigh."

"Leigh. Good morning my best friend in the whole wide world."

Just hearing her friend's voice made Leigh smile. "I wanted to call to apologize for not seeing you in time to stop you from leaving this morning. I was watching the kids going off to school." She smiled. "Josh has been wonderful for Cassie." Hearing silence on the other end, she continued, "You got away from me so quickly this morning."

"Leigh, I am so glad you called. I have been trying to make it over all weekend but have been delayed with work. I thought I would come over today and see what you've done with the place. Josh tells me it is really looking fine over there." Anita paused for a moment to catch her breath, "I am so happy to have you close."

Leigh could feel her heart pounding under her shirt as she got the nerve up to ask, "Anita, did you come for a visit this morning?" The tension swelled inside of her body. "I saw someone in my house while I was outside and thought it was you."

"It wasn't me. I wish it had been me. I'd have loved watching our kids going off to school. Back in our day did you ever think about us having kids going to Salyersville High together?"

Leigh bit her lip. "If you didn't come over this morning, then who could've it been?"

"I don't know, Leigh. I haven't been out of the house this morning." Silence marked the uneasiness they both were feeling. Anita asked, "Who could it have been? Anyone know you are back and wanting to visit?"

Leigh stopped swinging, feeling as if the breath had been knocked out of her. "I don't have a clue as to who my visitor was." Her voice faded away.

Anita could tell from the sound of Leigh's voice that she was disturbed about the incident. She had planned on visiting today anyway, might as well do it now. Her friend sounded upset. She had to make her move easier. "Well, it wasn't me visiting, but I'd like to be "the visitor." What do you have planned for the day? Have time for an old friend?"

Leigh smiled, forgetting for a moment the woman visitor. "I'd love to spend time with my best friend."

"I'll be over in a minute." Anita decided to drive even though she usually loved walking the road to the Howard Farm. Leigh sounded like she needed someone immediately. She jumped into the Range Rover and sped down the road.

Leigh stayed on the porch until her friend arrived. She

didn't think she was afraid. It just felt unnerving to walk back into the living room. And looking at the fireplace gave her the jitters. She understood Cassie a bit more now. She mustn't tell Cassie about this; she was already scared and allowing her imagination to run away with her.

Relief spread throughout her soul when she saw Anita drive up to the house. She ran the few steps to the front porch and gave Leigh a long loving hug. "It is so good to see you." The two clung to each other; going back to the days when they had been inseparable. "I still can't believe you have made your way back to Salyersville to live next door to me." Anita raised her hands above her head and shouted, "Life is good."

"I love you my friend. How are you doing? You look fabulous."

Anita pushed Leigh back to look at her and answered, "It's all that farm work; you just wait; it's the best gym ever." They both laughed.

"Speaking of gyms, let's have a girl day. We can go over to Linda Lou's shop and gossip all afternoon while we get our hair done--maybe a mani' and pedi' … what do you say?" Anita raised her eyebrows and motioned toward her vehicle.

Leigh laughed and was almost in the Rover before she remembered the cattle and horses that would arrive later. "I don't think I can go. I have cows coming for stalls this afternoon." She was genuinely disappointed. She looked at her friend not able to express how much she wanted to be free today.

Anita stood thinking, "Are they just bringing them for the stall today? I bet Kyle would come over and house them for us."

Leigh shook her head, "No, I can't do that. This is my first day of working the farm. I can't leave. But thanks for offering Kyle up for work." They both laughed; remembering all the times they had coerced him into doing something for them.

It was a sport for them. Just how much would it take to get Anita's boyfriend to do what they wanted. He always acted as if he was being forced but they knew he was glad to help. He was the kindest man she had ever met. Anita had done well. They had grown up with Kyle, and he never changed. He was true, honest, hardworking, handsome, and always, in love with his wife.

Anita realized she had lost this battle, so she changed strategies. "Okay, if you won't leave with me, I am staying with you." She started making her way to the front door. "I plan to spend some time with my best friend and new neighbor today, and that is exactly what I am going to do." She grabbed Leigh's arm and nudged her forward. "What can we get into here? Got any ice cream or let's bake a cake and eat every crumb!"

Leigh laughed. "We'll have the best day ever." As they walked into the living room, Leigh glanced over to the fireplace. "Anita, I still don't know what went on here this morning. I have to tell you; it was more than a little eerie."

Anita leaned on the mantle. "We'll find out what or who was here. Time will tell." she said. She gave her friend a reassuring smile, "But for today, don't worry about it. This is our day."

"Do you know how much I love you?" Leigh squeezed her friend's arm. "Come on, I want to show you what I've done with the house so far. I'm pleased with the changes I've made."

After a day of self-manicures and pedicures, baking cookies, listening to old records, discussing decorating, Anita's house, Anita's husband, Leigh's ex-husband, Cassie, Josh, their friendship, and all the gossip Anita could think of; the two saw a cattle truck and several horse trailers driving up the road.

Following along behind them was Mark's work truck with feed for the livestock. He filled the feeder bins and watched as the horses were put into their stalls followed by the cattle. In one afternoon, the barns had come alive. The two farm hands had worked hard and the barns were in tiptop shape.

Once everything was settled, Mark promised to be back with a load of hay. Anita turned to Leigh and smiled.

"We have danced around our lives all day and here you have kept this juicy bit hidden from me." Her eyes, questioned Leigh.

Leigh shook her head. "No, it can't be … not now … not with Cassie in such a bad state about her father." She frowned into the view of the barn, "I can't do that to her."

Anita dropped her head, "I understand. Have you told Mark?"

"Yes, he knows how it is, and we have agreed to be friends for now." Leigh gave her friend the smile she knew Anita wanted to see. Anita smiled back.

"Well, my chores are waiting." Anita looked at her old friend. "It has been a wonderful day, my friend." She gave Leigh a hug.

"It's the first of many. Next one will be at my house, okay?" Anita hugged Leigh as they walked back to Anita's Rover. "Let me know when you find out who came calling, okay?"

Leigh shook her head that she would. "It has been a wonderful day. Thanks for coming, Anita. I can't wait until we do it again." She looked at her friend, "What have I done all these years without you close to me?"

Anita pulled away from the house, and Leigh hesitated and shook off her apprehension and walked into her home. She wanted to hear about her daughter's first day of school. She had a snack ready for Josh and Cassie, including plenty of cookies. Just as she turned to go to the stove, she heard a truck pull up to the barn. It must be Mark with the hay. She peeked out of the window, and there was the handsome man from her past, Mark, stacking the hay in the barn. She rushed to the door and quickly made her way over to help with the unloading. Just as they finished, Josh and Cassie drove up.

Leigh looked closely, checking to see if Cassie was in a good mood or not. She was laughing. Relief washed over her. "So was it a good day?"

Cassie bounced out of the truck. "Yes, I had a good day. My classes are great, thanks to Josh. He helped me get the teachers I needed. We have lunch and study hall together." Cassie motioned toward Josh. "Most of the guys from our group have lunch with us." Cassie smiled at her mom. "I think I'm going to like this year."

Josh walked around the truck and smiled at Leigh. "She has a good schedule." He motioned toward the barn, "Looks as if you are open for business."

"Yes, we are. We have a barn full of cows and horses, plenty of feed, hay, and hopefully good workers." She glanced at Cassie.

"I have never been close to a horse or a cow, how am I going to be any help?"

Josh laughed. "I'll teach you." He looked at the stalls full of animals. "There is something addicting about working with living animals. You will love it." He grinned at Leigh, "I can tell."

It was Cassie's turn to laugh. "Are you sure about that?"

"We will see that I'm right." Josh became serious. "First, we need to make a schedule. Since I will be helping you; you can help me." He paused and then added, "It'll be practice of course." He sent a sly glance toward Cassie. She missed his humor; she was too busy trying to wrap her brain around this task. She was very serious about learning. Josh and Leigh both looked at Cassie and then at each other and burst out laughing. The laughter brought Mark around the corner of the barn.

"What's so funny?" he asked. Cassie's good humor was fading away with the addition of company. Mark seeing Cassie's expression change, bid his goodbyes and told Leigh he'd start her a bill.

"Thanks, Mark." Leigh hated treating him as just a business partner. He was one of her best friends. She'd give Cassie a little time before she approached the subject of Mark again. Cassie would have to come around.

It was getting late, and everyone had things to do this evening. Mark left and soon after Josh was driving up the road to his farm. "I like him, Cassie." Leigh smiled as the two walked toward the barn. "He has good parents; they are both my oldest friends."

Leigh slowed her walk to talk with her daughter; "Actually, Anita came over and spent the day with me today."

"Did you guys have a good day?" She smiled. She wanted her mom to have a good life, even if at times it didn't seem that way.

"We had a very good day." Leigh looked nostalgic, "I have missed my best friend. I'm glad I have her and Kyle back in my life." Leigh smiled at Cassie. "Let's look at our new family, shall we?"

"They are gorgeous Mom." Cassie shouted. She was so excited. She was going to get to be close to these beautiful animals every day.

"Okay, they have been fed, and the stalls are clean, let's go in and have some dinner." Leigh put her arm around her daughter's small waist and led her across the road to the house they were close to making their home. "What box of food would you like tonight; pizza rolls, mac and cheese, potato skins, you choose?" They laughed at their choices for dinner. They both knew the one thing Leigh hated was cooking. She grabbed the cookie platter and danced it in front of Cassie. "Homemade ... I swear ... I told you Anita came over."

Cassie snatched one from the platter, "These are just what I need." They ended up having a glass of milk and eating cookies. It was just the girls, who cared what they had for dinner.

"What a good day." Leigh declared. As they got ready for bed, Cassie asked to sleep with Leigh again. This situation was beginning to concern Leigh, but she didn't mention it to Cassie—not yet.

Nine

Cassie walked down the long hallway of "A" wing; making her way to German, her favorite class, when she saw Kari walking toward her. She painted a smile on her face.

"Hey, Kari, how are you?" Cassie tried to be pleasant with the girl that only days before had made her feel less than equal. She was determined to try again to be friends with her. After all, they were both from "The Creek" and had the same friends.

"I haven't seen you around school before, Kari."

Kari hesitated before coming to a complete stop. "Good thing, don't you think?" She gave Cassie a sly look. "We wouldn't want to burst your bubble now would we?"

Cassie wrinkled her forehead, "What are you talking about, Kari? What bubble do you mean?"

Kari gave a sideways glance at the tall skinny girl she was walking with and told her to go on to class; she would be there in a minute.

Cassie waited, curious as to what this girl could possibly say that would burst her bubble.

"Have you asked Josh how he feels about me?" Kari was so pleased with herself that she couldn't keep her face from showing her pleasure.

Cassie shot back, "Why would I ask?" She tried to hide the fact that she was getting nervous; it was hard not to be nervous around this girl. She was much more confident than anyone Cassie had ever met. She got whatever she wanted and right this minute she wanted to get at Cassie.

Kari smiled and moved closer to Cassie's face as if she were telling a good friend a secret. Only this conversation wasn't a friend telling another friend a secret; this was the enemy moving in for the kill and Kari's face displayed the game plan. "Have you asked Josh who he talks to every night before going to sleep?" Her eyes pierced Cassie's. "Do you really want a boyfriend who keeps secrets like that from you?" Satisfaction reflected on her face. "Don't be so naïve, Cassie." She smiled, "Josh and you just met, do you think he can get over me that fast?" All she had to do was bring it to an end. "Get real, girl, he is using you because I don't want him anymore." Again, she smiled her evil smile, "Welcome to Salyersville, Miss City." She walked away, and Cassie could hear her sharp laughter as she went into Ms. Chapman's biology class.

Cassie was rooted to the spot. That encounter had changed her world. Did she believe Kari? If this were really going on, wouldn't Sarah have warned her? What did she do with this information? Should she ask Josh or Sarah if it was true? She wasn't sure what the answer was, but she couldn't stay here; she was late for German.

After class, she spoke to no one. It was one time that being new and having no one notice you had been a good thing. She realized she didn't have a clue what happened in German class today. All she had done was replay the scene with Kari, her menacing face, her laughter, and what she had said.

Could Kari's stabbing words be true? How? Cassie thought of Josh's face; heard his laughter and couldn't believe he would keep this from her. He was always so truthful about everything.

Even so, Kari had seemed to be confident about her information, almost bragging about the situation. Why would Josh call Kari every night? He never called her before going to sleep. Was it because maybe, he was on the phone to his ex-girlfriend? Okay, this would eat her up if she didn't find answers. The best way to get past this was to confront Josh. She would ask him this afternoon on their way home. Only one more class to endure and then she would clear up this mess. As she walked into class, she saw Sarah waiting for her. She hesitated and then pasted on a smile while her insides were quivering.

Finally, the bell rang, and Cassie hurried to the truck

and waited for Josh. Kari strolled by and gave her an evil smile and waved. Cassie waved back, but the smile she had commanded her face to offer didn't quite materialize.

"Hey, pretty girl, ready to head home?" Josh called as he sprinted across the parking lot toward her. He grabbed her and lightly brushed a kiss on her lips. He jumped in the truck not waiting for a reply. She climbed in without saying anything. She felt so comfortable with Josh. He couldn't do this to her, could he? Maybe his mother forced him to be more than helpful, or was she unknowingly forcing herself on him? Whatever the reason, sneaking calls to your ex-girlfriend every night was just wrong on so many levels.

Josh turned the radio up a notch and in one quick move grabbed Cassie's hand. Their relationship had been easy and right. He looked over at her, and his cheery face became serious. "Cassie, what happened?" He searched her face for answers. "You don't look good." He paused. "Was it something at school? Talk to me."

Cassie arranged herself so that she could look at Josh's eyes as he drove his truck. She didn't want to miss anything in case he lied about something, she was sure she could tell by his facial expression. She took a deep breath and pushed forward. "I met Kari in the hallway before fifth period today." She looked hard and long at his face … nothing. Okay, this is good, no reaction. She continued. "She told me something that is extremely hard for me to believe or imagine as true." She took another deep breath and continued. "It's about you, Josh."

Josh's face became serious. "Cassie, Kari and I dated for over a year. It wasn't a good year, but she got under my skin." He looked deep into Cassie's eyes. "She is different in private than she is in a crowd of people. But, that was over long before you came to town. Whatever she told you, you have to know she and I are no more." He looked at Cassie; his look was deep and true, "I really care for you Cassie. You are the best thing to happen to me in a very long time. Whatever Kari said, please don't doubt that, okay? We go together so well; we are so comfortable with each other." Cassie looked into his eyes for a long minute before going on with what she had to say.

"I know we've had some good times. I think that our time together has been easy and natural, even comfortable for both of us. I realize that since our moms are best friends, it is understandable that you feel you must entertain me."

Josh laughed. "Do you really think I'd sport you around town as my girlfriend if I weren't interested in you?" He offered a half-grin. "If you had been ugly, you'd be dropped off at the entrance of the school or something." They both laughed.

"You could never be mean-hearted, even if I were ugly. You have a good heart, Charlie Brown." He smiled, and she gave him a peck on the cheek. "I still have to ask you something. Kari told me something, and I have to know if it is true." She looked at him anxiously, "Promise you won't hate me?"

"Never!" He dramatically reached for her hand and kissed it and held it to his heart. She giggled as she pulled her hand away. She moved again so she could see his face when she asked the question, although she was feeling much better about the answer now. Josh always made her feel better. She could feel her cheeks flush, and her heart was pounding. "Josh, Kari said you call her every night before going to sleep, is that true?" She watched as a flicker fleetingly moved over his face. Oh no, it was true. "Josh, please tell me that she lied." She pleaded, tears already welling up in her eyes. She refused to allow them to spill over.

Josh turned his head away as if he needed to look at something out his window for what seemed to be as long as the trip home. What was he doing? Was he trying to think of a good lie to tell her so she wouldn't be mad? Her nice life was tumbling around her as she sat in the truck listening to the loud silence. Until now, she'd never noticed the hum of the engine or the sound of the tires as they drove.

Unable to look at Josh, she whispered, "Okay, I have my answer."

She looked out the window to discover she was home, and as he pulled to a stop in front of the large walkway to her house, she whispered, "Thanks for the ride." As she jumped out of the truck, she thought she heard Josh calling her name, but her heart beat so loudly she wasn't sure. She willed herself to walk up the walkway and into the house without looking back.

Ten

She managed to wait until she was in the house before allowing the tears to come. How had she been so stupid as to think she could waltz into this hick town and find a boyfriend that was as perfect as Josh? Are all men scum? They either end up hurting you early in the relationship or years later. Life sucks. Today, she didn't even think of the goose bumps that normally covered her as she climbed up the stairs. She was just trying to get to her room before her mother saw her. She needed to get a good cry in before her mom called her for dinner.

She fell on the bed and the tears flowed. If she could fall asleep, she could forget her dreadful life. Sleep is what she did well when she was depressed. She had slept most of last year when her father not only moved out of the house, but also got married to another woman. Men, she hated them all. At some point during her meltdown she managed to fall asleep.

Cassie opened her eyes and for a moment forgot where she was, and then it all came flooding back. She sat up in her bed and noticed the light coming through the window from the full moon. She started to pull herself off the bed when she noticed from the corner of her eye a figure standing at the end of her bed. Her heart stopped. It was the lady Cassie had seen before, but this time she had on a black flowing dress with a matching hat. Cassie couldn't see her face clearly, although she felt the woman was staring at her. Cassie felt her bones ache from fear. She attempted calling to her mother, but no words came. If she could turn on the lamp next to her bed, maybe the woman would be gone—but, she couldn't move or speak. She wasn't sure how long this lasted. It could have been a minute or an hour. Neither she nor the figure moved.

Leigh called Cassie's name, but when she didn't hear an answer she climbed the stairs to check on her. Cassie watched the woman in black as she moved away from her bed and glided into the dressing room next door. Her mother opened the bedroom door to find her daughter white as a ghost and staring straight ahead.

"Are you okay? You look like you just saw a ghost." Cassie looked at her mom and then at the doorway to the dressing room.

"I think I did." She crawled off her bed and grabbed her mom's hand. "Let's go downstairs." Leigh looked at her with a puzzled look but walked out of the room and down the stairs without arguing.

"Okay, what happened?" Leigh knew her daughter well. She knew her survival method was to dismiss trouble by sleeping it away. Anita had called earlier asking what was going on. She said Josh came home upset. They agreed not to interfere, but Leigh had to help her daughter if possible.

"I don't know; I was sleeping, and when I woke, there was a lady dressed in black staring at me. She didn't move; she just stared. It was eerie." She looked at her mom. "You have to realize there is someone in this house, Mom."

Leigh felt the chills run up and down her spine. She wasn't ready to admit this. They couldn't move; their resources were maxed out and besides things were so good here. Cassie had actually begun enjoying life in the country. So, did they live with the ghost? This whole situation was too bizarre. "Honey, you were sleeping and upset." Cassie shot her a look.

Leigh lowered her eyes and confessed, "Anita called and said Josh was upset when he came home." Leigh searched Cassie's face for answers. "She wanted to know what happened between the two of you." Leigh shook her head trying to clear one situation out while allowing the other situation to enter. "Anyway, you were asleep when you thought you were awake." She tucked a lock of Cassie's blond locks behind her ear. "You were still dreaming." Leigh was holding her breath hoping that Cassie believed her. "Couldn't you have been dreaming?"

Cassie tried to fight the frustration she felt washing

over her body as she blurted. "NO! I was not DREAMING. There is a woman that haunts this house, Mother." Leigh had never seen her daughter this upset.

"Cassie, you need to calm down. Josh and you have had an argument, and you feel horrible. It will work itself out; give it time." She reached to give Cassie a hug and that is all it took. Cassie fell into her mother's arms and allowed herself to cry for Josh, for her father, for her life in Louisville, her friends, for her fears of this house, all of it. Leigh held her. She had needed this cry session for over a year now. Maybe the anger and hate would move out and allow her daughter to be her beautiful self again. Mother and daughter sobbed while clinging to each other.

After an hour of crying, Cassie sat up and decided that all the tears were gone. Crying hadn't given her any answers or made things any better; she was finished. What doesn't kill you makes you stronger. That's what everyone says. Cassie figured she must be one of the strongest people on earth after the year she had survived. She looked at her mother's tear stained face. "I'm finished crying."

"Good, now it's time for the ice cream." Leigh squeezed her daughter's hand. "Which box do you want?"

"BOX? Mom, we aren't getting a bowl?" Cassie giggled.

"Nope. Every crying-angry-hurt-at-boyfriend session ends with friends obliterating a box of ice cream." Leigh shot Cassie a look of love. "So which box do you want?"

Cassie gave in, "Butter Pecan sounds great." She allowed a free laugh that made her feel so much better. Leigh joined in and pulled out chocolate mint for herself. They walked arm in arm back to the living room and devoured the boxes of ice cream. Her mom had been right, she felt better.

"Mom, I can't go back up those stairs tonight." She faced her mother. She desperately needed her mother to know what was happening in the house. Leigh wasn't listening to the facts, dismissing every strange occurrence.

"I got your back, my girl." She leaned close to Cassie

and offered; "Sleep with me in my bed. It's not like there isn't enough room." She chortled.

Cassie grinned and hugged her mom. Her mother was one stubborn lady, but she loved her, and she knew that when all was said and done her mom would do anything for her best interest. Cassie appreciated her mother for not prying into her and Josh's situation. She had the best mother, ever.

Eleven

The next morning Cassie got dressed early. She had decided to ride the bus to school. Others did it, why couldn't she? She made her way out the door just in time to catch the bus as it labored over the road going to other stops for pickups. Cassie climbed up the steps and found a seat near the front. They all sat silent in their own thoughts as they moved down the highway. The smell of sweaty bodies and old vomit permeated her senses. OMG what was this? How do people ride these things every day? Wait, she would know in a little while; she would be one of those people. As she sat staring blankly out the window, she saw the Chevy truck coming up beside the bus. It was Josh. He was alone, and he didn't look happy. Life sucked.

After an hour of riding on the dinosaur of filth, Cassie climbed off the bus. Students crowded through the entrance of the school, making their way to class. Cassie joined other students pushing through the crowd, trying to find her locker before going to class.

Sarah was standing beside her locker waiting for Cassie, but she couldn't talk about Josh—not yet. The hurt was too raw. She greeted Sarah, and as Sarah began to discuss what had happened yesterday, Cassie held up her hand as a sign of stop and stated, "I can't talk about this right now. Please, Sarah, leave it alone for a while." She frowned and walked away blindly making her way to her first class, Geometry. The last thing she wanted was to lose her good friend just because it wasn't working with Josh. She'd find Sarah during the next break and ask for her forgiveness. She just couldn't discuss Josh and Kari right now. She prayed Sarah would understand.

Lunch loomed over Cassie like a black cloud. This would be the first time she would see Josh since the fight.

She wasn't sure how to handle it, but it was coming, and she would have to think on her feet. She decided to take the situation as it presented its self. With no real plan, she entered the lunchroom and scanned the table. No Josh. She didn't want him to feel he couldn't be with his friends. She turned and walked out of the lunchroom. She found a bench outside and sat alone. All she was thinking about was how miserable she was and how miserable she had made Josh. He had tried to be nice to her because their mothers were good friends, and she had gone overboard. She wrinkled her forehead; he didn't have to kiss me ... I didn't ask him to, he just did it. Why did he do it, to make Kari jealous? It wouldn't be the first time someone had been used to make another jealous.

She pulled out the new novel she had been reading and pretended to read. No one bothered to speak, thinking she was immersed in her book when the truth was; she couldn't focus on anything. All she saw was Josh's face when she asked if he called Kari every night before going to sleep. If he cared that much for her, why didn't they just get back together? It wasn't as if she had caused the breakup.

Just as she began gathering her things for the next class, Sarah appeared. "There you are. Cassie, you have to listen to me."

Cassie rushed to gather her things in order to escape. "Stop running." Sarah stepped in front of Cassie in order to see her face. "Josh is miserable." She hesitated, giving Cassie time to react. "I don't know what you guys fought about, but you have to talk with each other. I've never seen two people more miserable in my life. Promise me you will talk." Sarah demanded.

Cassie grinned at her, promising that at some point, she and Josh would talk. She left for her next class. She didn't see any of the gang for the rest of the day. Kari wasn't around either. Was Josh with Kari? She had to stop this jealousy. Lovely, her last class and then a wonderfully scented tour of Lick Creek on a school bus. Followed by an evening entertaining some ghost that was taking over her house. Oh, how she missed her old home and her old friends.

The bus ride home was unbearable. She was tired, hungry, heartbroken, and sad. In addition to the bumpy winding road and the stench of the bus, she shared it with people who seemed to be miserable too.

She tried to forget where she was by staring out the window. She unconsciously gazed at all the cows grazing in the pastures, the horses running, and the fields of crops. It was hard to keep her mind off of Josh. As the bus turned onto Lick Creek road, Cassie saw the pickup. It was Josh. He was alone in the truck. Cassie wasn't sure why she was so happy about this, but she couldn't deny that she was happy. She tried to get a look at his face when he turned, and their eyes met. Was it sadness she saw or pity for an idiot that had assumed too much from him? No, it was sadness.

The source of his sadness wasn't clear, but she knew him well enough to know that he was not happy. The bus moved up the road while Josh followed behind. Cassie hated that he would see her get off this thing. As the bus slowly found her house, she readied herself for the embarrassment that lay ahead. "Brace yourself, Cassie Ward. You can do this."

As she stepped off the bus, she noticed Josh's truck wasn't behind them anymore. Hopefully, he had gone around the bus, and she wouldn't have to face the embarrassment. The bus pulled away, and she started walking toward the porch of her house. Once the bus had pulled over the hill, she saw him. The truck was parked over by the barn. He was taking long strides toward her. She felt faint and flushed at the same time. What to say? She stopped and waited for the disaster that was going to happen in a few moments.

He looked down in her face and simply stated, "I'm sorry, you have to listen to me, please." His eyes were full of pain. Cassie could hear the stress in his voice.

She didn't say anything. Thoughts or words didn't enter into her brain at the moment. She would do as he requested; she would listen.

Josh led her to the swing on the porch. He started to hold her hand and then stopped. He pulled his hand back while he cleared his throat. "Cassie, I have to tell you the whole story. Once you have heard me out; you decide what you want." He stopped long enough to offer a forlorn look of pleading, "Cassie, you have to know that I really like you. I have liked you since the day I saw you walking toward my farm." He hesitated, looked in her eyes and took a deep breath. "I don't want to mess things up," he pleaded.

"When Kari told you about me calling her every night, she technically told you the truth. I did call her, but not for the reason she hinted." He waited for a moment as if to gain the courage to go on with his explanation. "I can't tell you everything, but you have to know it was a life or death situation. I felt I had no other choice." Again, he stopped to evaluate Cassie's reaction. When he couldn't determine her feelings, he pulled his eyes away and proceeded.

"I've talked with the counselors at school, and they are dealing with the issue. I refuse to shoulder that guilt anymore." He turned on the swing so that his whole body faced Cassie, "I promise you there will never be any more calls to Kari's house, whether you agree to see me anymore or not."

Cassie just stared with a crease between her eyes. What did he just say? She wasn't sure if he said anything or not. She tried to digest it one more time before she spoke. She looked at Josh and willed him to look at her. His face was full of anguish. He was hurting, whatever he was saying. Cassie finally asked, "Will you tell me that again? I don't have a clue what you just said."

Josh looked at her and smiled. "I'm sorry, Cassie. I am truly sorry this mess has happened." He looked deep into her eyes and declared, "I want you to know, I have never even thought of another girl since you came to town." He looked up and smiled at her again. "I want you to be the only girl for me." He searched her face, "Will you be my girlfriend?"

Cassie looked stunned and repeated, "I don't know what you just told me, Josh." Cassie was just as confused as she had been before their talk. "Why did Kari tell me you called her every night? I need to know Josh." She saw the dark disappointment spread over his face. She searched his face for answers as she asked, "Wouldn't you want to know if it were the other way around?"

Josh ducked his head, "Yes, I would want to know. That's why this is so hard for me; I can't tell you all the details … not now anyway. All I can say is please trust me when I say I have not or never will do you wrong." He took a chance and pulled Cassie's hand into his own. "Please believe me. I feel we've gotten so close in such a short time. I don't want this to end."

Cassie still felt numb. Why couldn't he tell her? What had he said, 'life and death'? What did that mean? She gazed at the porch floor and finally raised her head to find Josh staring at her with the most anguished face she had ever seen. "Josh, will you give me a little time to figure this out? I'm having a hard time wrapping my brain around why you can't explain calling your ex-girlfriend every night." She released her jagged breath and offered, "I promise as soon as I get this worked out in my mind I'll give you a call." She looked at him pleadingly as he met her eyes with his.

He agreed to wait. He awkwardly rose from the swing and told her he hoped he'd see her soon. They both smiled, and he turned and was gone. Cassie sat on the swing for a long time. She wanted to believe him but what had he asked her to believe. She was half mad at him for putting her in this situation.

She made herself go inside. Her mother was waiting for her in the kitchen. She had made hot chocolate. She handed Cassie a mug and without asking even one question, hugged her daughter. Cassie felt safe in her mother's arms. She allowed her day to melt away. She wanted to tell her mother about Josh, but she couldn't bear to talk about it. "Mom, can we talk in the morning?"

"Of course we can." Leigh caressed her daughter's face. "Let's go to bed and sleep on it. Are you bunking in with me, partner?"

"Do you mind?"

"Of course not. Ready to go now?"

"Yes, it's been a long day." Cassie pulled a face. "Riding on a bus for at least two hours a day is exhausting." They both laughed as they headed for the big four-poster bed.

Twelve

Just as they snuggled into the comfort and warmth of their grandparents' soft bed, they heard a hair-raising noise in the kitchen. "What was that?" cried Cassie.

Leigh had already leaped from the bed and was racing out of the room. "I don't know." She held her hand up as if to protect her daughter, "You stay here, Cassie."

Cassie was not about to stay in this freaking house by herself. She raced behind her mother until without warning Leigh stopped. Cassie plowed into her, and they both went tumbling into the kitchen. Once she was in the kitchen, Cassie saw what had made her mom stop so abruptly. Scattered over the kitchen floor were all the cabinet drawers and their contents.

Leigh tried to control her voice but barely contained a shriek. "What the heck just happened?" Both of them felt scared and ready to run. Leigh couldn't believe her eyes. Her grandparents had given her a home. There was just one problem. The ghosts that lived in her newly acquired home didn't want them here. "Okay. I give up." She fought to control her emotions. "We have a problem, and I don't know what to do about it." Leigh began to cry.

Finally, Cassie gained her voice back and reasoned, "Mom, we have known there are funny things going on in this house ever since we moved in here. And, whatever it is, it hasn't hurt us yet; let's just go to bed." After gathering her nerves, she wanted to make sure her mother didn't try to explain this event away. "But, Mom, we have to find out what is going on in this house. We need to find the source of this stuff." She looked demanding at her mother, "Okay, Mom?"

Leigh straightened herself and gained her composure. "Okay, we need to collect ourselves." Cassie could see the mother she had known her whole life begin to work through the situation. "We have something going on and need to find out why this is happening." She looked at Cassie, almost without seeing her. "You're right, Cassie; we have not been hurt with whatever is happening here." Leigh bent down to pick up the lids to Grandma's pots and pans; and then collected the rest of the stuff. They finished cleaning in silence. Once the evidence of what had happened was gone, Leigh took Cassie's hand, and they went back to bed. Cassie marveled because she wasn't scared anymore. She was glad her mom finally gave in and acknowledged that there were eerie events happening in their home.

The next morning, when Cassie came into the kitchen for her cereal, her mom sat at the dining table. She was cuddling her coffee, so intent on her thoughts that she hardly noticed her daughter. Cassie understood her mother's mood. She had gone through her own moments of trying to understand what was happening in this house. She smiled and put on her cheerful face. "Good morning, Mom."

"Oh, good morning, Baby. How did you sleep?" Leigh pulled her thoughts back to the present. She looked at her daughter and saw dark circles under her eyes. Her heart broke. What had she done? She'd made her daughter leave the only home she knew in order to come to a home that was scaring both of them. How could they make this their home?

Cassie chirped, "Fine and fiddle. Isn't that what Granddad always said?"

Leigh laughed, "Yes. He did say that. He would say that every morning."

Cassie joined in with a genuine snicker, "How could he be so happy every day?" She smiled thinking of her great-grandparents. Leigh looked over at Cassie; her grandparents wanted Cassie to enjoy the farm, and it was their gift to the two of them. She wanted so badly to make it work here...for Cassie. But, she would not have her daughter in danger. She had to find out what was happening without people thinking she was off her rocker.

"He also said, 'make it a great day or not—the choice is yours.' Do you remember?"

"I remember!" Cassie smiled at the thought. "At the time, I never paid much attention to his little sayings but what great messages. Granddad, the Gandhi of Lick Creek." They both laughed.

"Mom, I think I should tell you, I haven't disliked living here. It has been so different from what I thought it would be like." Cassie tried to explain, "I love the cattle and horses." She tried again, "And I'm getting new friends."

Leigh loved her daughter; she had grown into a mature young woman. "And, what about Josh? Where does he fit in the picture?" Leigh watched as a dark shadow moved over her daughter's face. It was obvious that there were problems with the new lovebirds. "What happened, Cassie?"

"I'm not sure, Mom." Cassie's face grew deeper while she tried to find a way to explain to Leigh what Josh had asked her to accept. How do you explain something like this and make it seem normal? She took a deep breath. She was going to try; she needed someone to help her digest this, and she would have to admit her mom had always had a good reasonable head. She took a deep breath again and said, "Here goes."

"The other day at school, Kari, Josh's old girlfriend that he hasn't dated since last school year, stopped me in the hallway and told me I didn't really know Josh. She said I needed to ask Josh who he calls every night before he goes to sleep. She said they talked every night." She stole a peek at her mom just to see how she was taking this information.

Leigh seized the pause and offered, "Sounds like a jealous girl that wasn't ready to move on after a breakup. You didn't take what she said to heart without talking to Josh, did you?"

Cassie shook her head no and mumbled, "No, I asked him about it that afternoon." Leigh could see the pain plastered on Cassie's face. "He didn't deny it."

"That's the day you decided to take a long nap

upstairs." Cassie nodded.

"Honey, you two have to talk. You need to understand what is going on. It sounds like you have a jealous girl that is trying to break the two of you up, and you are allowing her. Josh doesn't seem to be the type of boy to play the game of seeing two different girls. Talk to him."

Cassie lowered her head even more than she already was, "We did talk, last night."

Leigh searched Cassie's head; she tried to find her face, but she had it so buried in her cereal that she couldn't see her. "And?"

Cassie took another deep breath, "He said it was true, they did talk every night but that it wasn't what Kari led me to believe. He said it was a matter of life or death and that he had discussed it with the counselors at school. He said he had washed his hands of the situation." She raised her head to look at her mother; she wanted to get her first reaction to what she was going to tell her next. "He said he couldn't give me an explanation of why he had called her every night and that I'd have to believe him for the moment." She waited.

Leigh took her cue. "This doesn't sound like a love affair to me." Leigh was seriously weighing the information her daughter had given her. "Why can't he tell you what was going on, did he say?"

Cassie shook her head no. "He just said he liked me and wanted to date only me. He said that he hadn't, and wouldn't be making any more phone calls." Cassie looked at her mother and concluded, "I told him I'd have to process all of this since I didn't and couldn't know why he was calling her every night." She rose from her seat, "That's why I am riding the bus again this morning, and here it comes. I got to go. See you tonight, Mom." She hugged her mom and ran to the road just in time to jump on the bus.

Cassie wondered again what Josh meant by "life and death,"--was this girl threatening him? Did Anita know about this? Would her mom call Anita? No, Cassie knew her mom would wait until she had more information.

She knew her mom was proud of her for riding the bus. She wasn't "giving in" to the situation.

Cassie thought about her mom at the kitchen table, having her first cup of coffee and trying to sort through what had happened last night in the kitchen. How could she explain it? If it had only been the utensils from the drawers or only one drawer, but it wasn't, it was ALL of the drawers and ALL of the contents that were scattered all over the kitchen floor. It was a mystery to both of them, but Cassie was beginning to develop a theory; every time she saw something, or they heard something, it happened in a room that was being redecorated. Maybe that had something to do with it. She never thought she would be considering that her house was haunted. She didn't believe in the paranormal—at least not until now.

Leigh had told Cassie that she didn't think Josh was interested in another girl. "Anyone watching him when he is around you Cassie would know he was smitten." Her concern had been his comment about "life and death"… that was a significant burden. And, whose life and whose death was he talking about?

Leigh always told her she was "wise beyond her years." Cassie just hated to go through the journey of finding out the answers; bus rides, doubts of someone you felt comfortable with, more bus rides. Life was hard sometimes.

Leigh had decided to try an experiment with the house. Since the events were beginning to happen in the kitchen, she thought she would start redecorating it full-force today. She would provoke the unwelcome lady of the house.

Maybe the country air was making her crazy. She drug all of her supplies into the kitchen and began stripping the cabinets and sanding. Surely she could get a bite from all of this mess. She worked throughout the day while Cassie was at school. Not one sound; nothing flung across the room; no one came for a visit, just her and the radio. Okay, she tried. At least she had a good start on the kitchen.

After Leigh had finished working on the kitchen for the

day, she decided she would visit Uncle Ray and Aunt Betty. Maybe they could shed some light on what was happening with the house. She would have to be discreet. She didn't want her Uncle and Aunt to think she had gone crazy.

She hopped out of the Explorer and made her way to one of the barns on Uncle Ray's farm. Sure enough, she found both him and Aunt Betty admiring the new cow Uncle Ray had just purchased. Aunt Betty called for her to come join them. Leigh obliged. Uncle Ray asked how things were coming on the farm. "Do you need anything done over there? I'd be glad to come over and lend a hand."

Leigh shook her head. She wanted to steer the conversation toward the house, so she began telling the two about the work she had been doing on the house. Aunt Betty was excited about the kitchen renovations. Uncle Ray listened but didn't seem as interested in the house as he was with the farm running smoothly.

Leigh attempted to pull him into the conversation again. "Funniest thing happened last night." Leigh gauged the reaction of her aunt and uncle. "After Cassie and I had gone to bed, we heard the loudest noise coming from the kitchen." She watched as Uncle Ray began to listen to every word. Aunt Betty's face filled with fright.

"What happened to make the sound?" Aunt Betty asked. Uncle Ray shook his head. Betty was visibly distraught.

Satisfied she had their full attention, Leigh continued. "When we went to investigate the noise we found the kitchen in shambles. The cabinet drawers were scattered all over the floor, and the utensils and pots and pans were strewn all over. We didn't know what to think about the mess. What do you think would cause that to happen Uncle Ray?"

Ray didn't give an answer. He seemed to be weighing what Leigh had just told him. "Leigh, that house has had unexplainable things happening in it ever since Mom and Dad moved in there. They never figured out what was going on or at least they never told us if they did."

Leigh changed the conversation back to the new addition to their herd. She had all the information Uncle Ray could give her, and she didn't want him to worry about Cassie and her. Even when Uncle Ray followed her lead and began telling Leigh about his new purchase, Aunt Betty's face was still frozen with anxiety.

Leigh bid her Uncle and Aunt good-bye claiming she needed to get home before Cassie made it home from school. Aunt Betty called after her, "Be careful in that house." Leigh heard the two of them discussing the house as she pulled out of the drive.

Thirteen

Cassie thought the bus ride would never end. It was worse than the day before. She stepped off the bus just in time to see the back of Josh's head going up the stairs toward the entrance of the school. Her first instinct was to call to him to wait for her, but she caught herself. She would leave him alone for the time being. She'd promised him she would call him when she came to terms with the situation. As of yet, she couldn't get her mind to reason out what she should or shouldn't do about all of this. No, she would wait. It wouldn't be fair to her or to Josh if she pretended everything was fine when she wasn't sure. She climbed the stairs and slowly walked to first period, Mr. Parnell and Algebra, her worst subject.

At the end of the day, she found herself longing to find Josh's truck and escape from the yellow, stinky monster that sat parked in wait for its victims. She stared at the bus while it waited with its open mouth, ready to eat her up and spit her remains out by her front door once she had been abused and used. Alas, she would force herself to stay on the route to the huge yellow mouth and only take a couple of longing peeks at the Chevy waiting, inviting her to come enjoy the ride home. She couldn't wait until next year when she was old enough to drive herself; the yellow monster could find someone else to attack.

By the time Cassie made it home she was sick to her stomach from the fumes and the stench of sweaty bodies. Why did she have to live so far away from school? She had walked to school when she lived in Louisville. Now it took two hours of her day just to endure a horrific ride to and from school.

After she was finished with the hell-ride, she had to face going back to the house, the house that was trying to scare her away. What a lovely life she had found herself living. She turned away from the house and strolled over to the barn. She might as well get her chores done early. Maybe the animals could help her work through the emotions she was feeling towards Josh. Josh, the one good thing about this place. Everyone was friendly with her, but she knew they were Josh's friends, and they were friendly to her because of him. Although, she knew her new friends were true friends, she was certain that their loyalty was with Josh. Even Sarah who had made a point to have lunch with her every day would choose Josh if push came to shove.

Sarah declared that both Josh and Cassie were her friends and she refused to believe that they couldn't work out their differences. She was determined to make Cassie feel better. Cassie was so happy that Sarah was there to be her friend. Sarah believed Josh was innocent of what Kari accused him of doing…her words. Cassie smiled when she remembered Sarah's face as she professed, "Josh cares for you Cassie. I've never seen him so happy as when you two are together. Don't allow Kari to ruin this for you."

Cassie had agreed with Sarah. Josh had seemed happy when they were together. Cassie couldn't help but think it was more than just happy; they were so comfortable and connected with each other. She could not believe Josh would do something that horrible to her.

She emptied the pail of feed into the trough for the last cow. She watched as the cow slowly moved closer to the feed and began eating. She decided at that moment that she DID believe Josh. She wanted more than anything to give him another chance. She couldn't get past the secret he was keeping, but hopefully he would feel free to tell her what was going on with Kari.

She couldn't wait until she got back to the house; she found her backpack and purse she had laid beside the barn and pulled out her cell phone. She took a deep, loud, nervous breath and punched in Josh's number. She heard Josh's voice in only two rings. "Josh, its Cassie."

"Yea, I could tell that voice anywhere."

She smiled. "It's good to hear your voice." She couldn't think of what to say next. The silence was thick over the phone.

Josh cleared his throat and broke the silence. "So, have you come to any decision about us?" Silence filled the phones. "I hope this is good news, Cassie. I miss you."

"I miss you too," Cassie whispered. She had never had a boy to affect her in this way. She genuinely cared for him. "Josh, I want this, whatever it is between us, to work." She quickly added, "I am still having a hard time with the secrecy between Kari and you." She made her voice as firm as she possibly could. "If you can tell me that, at some point, I will learn why you felt you needed to talk with her every night, I can wait to find out the reason."

"I'd like nothing more than to tell you right now. It is killing me to keep this from you, but I can't discuss it—not yet." He waited and when he didn't hear from Cassie he continued. "As soon as I possibly can, I will tell you everything, I promise."

Silence.

"Cassie?"

"Yes?"

"May I come over? I want to see you right now!"

Cassie smiled into the phone. "I want to see you too."

"I'm almost finished with the chores, and then I am on my way. And Cassie?"

"Yes."

"I am so happy."

"Me too, Josh." They both laughed, ending their phone call. Cassie rushed from the barn searching for her mom. She needed to tell her what she had decided. She knew her mom would be glad; she liked Josh. She entered the house prepared to yell her mom's name when she was greeted with a teary eyed Leigh. "Mom, what is wrong?" She dropped next to her mother.

"I've thought about this house all day, Cassie. I can't risk your safety." She looked at her daughter with tears streaming down her face. "I have decided we are leaving this house and going back to the city."

Cassie felt numb. Wasn't this what she had wanted from the moment she had learned they were moving to Salyersville? Why was she screaming on the inside? She was just getting settled in this life. What about Josh? She was not ready to give up Josh. She couldn't believe that she was thinking this, but she no longer wanted to leave.

"Mom, I don't want to leave here. I have just found good friends, and I have Josh." Cassie moved near to her mother. "My life here is getting good, and I don't want to lose it now." She tried to reason with her mother. "This house isn't hurting us. We don't even know what is going on with it, why are we running?" Cassie felt the tears burn her eyes. She thought about the farm, the cows, the horses, and all the work her mom had put into the house. "We can't leave…Mom?"

"Cassie, do you think I want to take us back to Louisville? I want to stay here too, but I can't put you in danger." Leigh squared her shoulders, something she did when she had made up her mind; and when she had there was no changing her. "We both realize that something is going on in this house. I'm scared for you to stay here." Leigh caressed her daughter's hand. "Please see it from my point of view."

When Josh got to the house, both Cassie and Leigh were sobbing on the couch. Josh knocked on the door expecting to see a happy Cassie, but instead he saw a red-eyed, flushed face with tears spilling down. "What is the matter?"

Josh stepped inside holding on to Cassie. His first reaction was to protect her from whatever had made her cry. Once in the house he was alarmed to find Cassie's mom also crying. Had the two been in a terrible fight? Was it because of him? He turned to face Leigh, "Do I need to leave?"

Leigh began laughing through the tears, "I am so sorry, Josh. Of course, you don't have to leave." She flashed a smile, "Cassie and I have to make some serious and tough decisions. Please, Josh, come in. It is so good to see you." Leigh wiped the tears away from her face and added, "I'm happy things are working out for you two."

Josh was on edge about the scene in front of him. He felt uncomfortable. Cassie held out her hand, and he held on as she led him to the couch. They sat down, and Leigh announced she was going to the kitchen to pop some popcorn for them. Once she left the room, Josh had reached over to Cassie and pulled her face close to him. He looked into her eyes and lightly kissed her lips. "I have missed you, Cassie Ward." He whispered.

He could feel Cassie sobbing even harder. "What is going on, Cassie? Did someone die?"

"No, it's hard to explain." How did she tell Josh that their house was haunted, and her mother was making her move away? She just spent the last few days away from him, and she felt as if she had lost her best friend. From what Sarah had told her he was not doing any better. How could this be happening again?

"Oh, Josh. I'm so sorry to have to tell you this, but Mom just told me that we are moving back to Louisville." She pulled her tear filled eyes up to meet his dreading what she would find. She had predicted that Josh would be hurt, and the pain he had on his face told her she had been correct. She held his eyes with hers for as long as they both could until he reached over and pulled her near him.

"You can't leave. I have just gone through the worst week of my life because I thought I had lost you. You can't leave." He pulled her closer as if holding on to her would make it all go away. Silence filled the room and then abruptly, as if he had just thought of it, "Why would you move when the farm is just beginning to succeed?" He pushed her back so he could look at her face, searching for answers.

Leigh had stopped in the dining room when she heard their conversation. The decision was killing her. The last thing she wanted was to move, but she could not put her daughter in danger. She didn't know what to do about the abnormal happenings. Her heart was tearing apart when she overheard Josh's question. She didn't want anyone to know what was happening with the house. If people found out Cassie and she would be laughed out of town instead of scared out of it. She didn't know what Cassie would say about the move, but she couldn't take a chance that she would tell Josh, so she barged in on the couple with the excuse of delivering popcorn.

Cassie looked relieved when her mother entered the room; Josh looked serious. Cassie's face was tear stained and Josh's looked like he'd just lost his best friend. What a sight. She had to answer for Cassie so Josh wouldn't ask her any questions.

Leigh sat down and looked at the both of them for a moment before she began. "I am so sorry; this is the last thing I wanted to happen. My old job has offered me my job back with a sizable raise in salary." She rushed to add, "I can't refuse." She looked at Cassie, her face empty of pain and replaced with confusion and then understanding. Josh looked at her with disbelief. She tried again. "The farm is hard work, and we are just two women with a couple of work hands trying to keep this place going. I can't expect Cassie to work as hard as we would have to work once we get to complete capacity."

Josh looked relieved, "I can help Cassie. Please, I can help her every evening to get things fed and ready for the night. I'd love helping out, Mrs. Ward." He was pulling out all stops. 'Mrs. Ward' was a nice touch.

Leigh could feel both Josh and Cassie's eyes piercing her. Each had their reasons, Josh wanting to see an agreement from her and Cassie wanting to see answers to why she was telling this lie to Josh. Leigh sat back; she wasn't lying. When she had called Humana and agreed to come back, she was offered a new position, one that paid more than her old position. She raised her face, as if she were a fighter, ready to take the last blow, "I am so sorry."

She didn't wait for the aftermath; she moved from her seat and made her way back to the kitchen where she cried harder than she had cried since her parents' deaths. Try as hard as she might she couldn't stop the sobs. She was so glad Cassie was preoccupied with Josh in the living room. She needed this time alone. She had been so happy when the lawyer had called telling her that her grandparents had left her the farm. It was perfect. She was depressed and angry with her ex-husband. Everything and everyone in Louisville made her think of their lives together. It was hard enough that he left her for his partner at work and married the day after their divorce, but everyone they knew was buzzing about it.

She couldn't go out of the house without someone asking her about what had happened. And, just before she had received the call from granddad's lawyer, her best friend at work, Jenny, had pulled her aside at lunch to tell her that Jack and Susan were having a baby. So when the call came it was literally heaven sent. Granddad and Grandma had saved her. She didn't think twice about the move. Cassie was angry with her, but her gut told her that Cassie would come around, and she had.

Now, just when they were getting it together, they had to leave this house. Why was this happening? What was going on with the house? According to Aunt Betty and Uncle Ray, her grandparents experienced some of the same things Cassie and she were experiencing.

She listened for voices in the living room, but all was silent. She made her way back to the dining room with the pretense of collecting the fallen popcorn from the floor. She spied into the living room, and her heart broke at the sight.

Josh and Cassie sat hugging, not moving, not talking. They sat clinging to each other, allowing their thoughts to blend in the silence. What had she done? They looked so happy together. Then, she remembered the kitchen floor with the cabinet drawers scattered to and fro. No, she couldn't and wouldn't risk Cassie's safety.

Fourteen

Josh glanced at the clock and was surprised that Leigh hadn't announced it was time for him to go home. He tugged at Cassie allowing her to move away only slightly. He held her close while he told her it was time he went home. They both had school tomorrow. "You are not gone yet, and I'm going to do everything I can to stop you from moving." He stroked her hair. "We have to fight this, Cassie; you cannot move away from me." She tried to not be sad when she looked back into his face, but she was sad. She didn't want to go anywhere, ghost or no ghost.

She was angry with the lady that had troubled them since they had moved in the house. I'm not going to allow her to ruin my life; I refuse. She looked back at Josh, but this time the sadness was gone. She was determined that she could stop her mom from ruining her life, especially with Josh's help. This move was not going to be a repeat of the last time her mother decided to move. Things had changed. Cassie had changed. She did not want to go back; it was too late. Salyersville, more importantly, Howard Farm was her life now. She and her mom wanted this life. She and Josh just had to convince her that they needed to stay here.

Josh kissed her one more time and promised they would create a plan of action tomorrow. They would not allow this to happen. They had almost lost each other and had learned how much they meant to each other. They were not going to be pulled apart because of some crazy job in Louisville.

He had watched Leigh with the animals. It was obvious that she was having the time of her life. He was confident that he and Cassie could change Leigh's mind. From what he'd witnessed with mother and daughter, he knew that Leigh would do anything to make sure Cassie was happy. And, he wouldn't hesitate to use this fact to persuade Leigh to stay on the Howard farm.

Cassie walked him to the door and with one last sweet kiss he was gone. Cassie turned to go search for her mother. She had to change her mind about this move. She could not leave Josh or her friends. She didn't know when it had happened, but she loved living on this farm with the animals and the people, especially the people, the next-door neighbors to be exact. "Mom, where are you?"

Leigh came from the kitchen with her head down. She hated to do this to her daughter just when they both were getting acclimated to their new life. She braced herself for what she knew was coming.

Cassie looked at her mother and without a word; she sat down, feeling defeated before she began her pitch for staying in Salyersville. Leigh smiled at her daughter. It wasn't the usual smile; this one was a sad 'I know baby, but it is going to happen' smile. Cassie opened her mouth, but nothing came out. She thought the tears were all cried out but there they were flowing down her face. "Please Mom, don't do this to us. Please." By the time she got the words out, she was sobbing.

Leigh laid her arm around her shoulders. "I wish we didn't have to, Sweetie, but we can't risk our safety just to live in this town." Leigh felt so frustrated and angry at the house. "I wish there was another answer, but you and I know what has happened in this house." Leigh warned Cassie about talking about the house to others. "And, Cassie, I think we should keep the reason for our move a secret. I am not sure anyone would believe us if we told them what has been happening."

Cassie stopped her tears long enough to look into her mother's face. Was she serious? How could they not tell anyone? If she didn't tell Josh, she wouldn't be any better than he was with the Kari issue. She refused to do that to Josh. "Mom, I will tell Josh. I am sorry, but I want him to know why I have to leave him, just when we found each other."

Leigh frowned, "Cassie, do you think Josh will understand this situation?"

"Probably not, since the one thing that we both want is for me to live here so that we can discover if what we have is real or not." Cassie stared her mother down. She was beginning to get the old familiar dislike for her that she had felt throughout the past year.

Leigh felt the chill coming on and resisted the instinct to pull away. She knew why Cassie was feeling this way, but she felt robbed of her daughter's love because of events out of her control. All she wanted was to make Cassie happy and instead she kept causing her to grieve. She didn't know how to make things right.

"Let's go to bed and sleep on this, okay?" Leigh gave way to her daughter as much as she dared without lying to her about their future move. Cassie heard the hint of a waver in her mother's stubborn resolve and decided it was enough to feel hopeful. Maybe there was something she could do to stop her mom this time around. She would tell Josh tomorrow, and the two of them would fight this together.

Just having a plan made her feel better. "Okay, let's go to bed." She had to make her mother believe she was brave enough to stay in the house. "I think I'm going to my room, Mom." She didn't give her time to argue; she headed for the stairs. Without allowing herself time to think, she made her way up to her bedroom. She was so angry at whatever was in their house that she didn't even care if something happened. She walked over to her bed and plopped down, whispering, "Bring it on!" Nothing happened. Maybe it was gone. She could only hope. She pulled down the bedding and slid into the comfy bed. "This room could be great if it wasn't so crowded in here," She mumbled to herself.

It had been a long, hard day. She was happier than she had been for the past few days and yet she was the saddest she had been since her mom had told her they were moving here. She lay down expecting the events of the past days to dance in her mind and yet within minutes;

she was sound asleep.

Leigh didn't have the same luck with sleep. She lay awake most of the night, while thinking through all the scenarios of the past month. She watched Cassie blossom when she was with Josh. She knew that her daughter was beginning to love the animals on the farm, and that was Leigh's hope for her.

Yet, she could see the lady standing next to her mantle and all of the unexplainable noises, along with the sight of her kitchen strewn with pots, lids, and all the utensils along with the drawers from the cabinets. They had not been hurt but would it get worse? She was scared for her daughter. She lay in her grandparents' bed ready at a moment's notice to leap up the stairs to her daughter's side. She thought of Mark. Secretly she had wished they could find their friendship again. Now, that wasn't going to happen. And, what about her best friend, Anita? They were finally close enough to be best friends once again. She was Josh's mom.

She looked over at the clock; it was only an hour before she had to get Cassie up for school. Obviously, she was not going to sleep tonight. She decided to rise early. She went to the kitchen and made herself a strong cup of coffee and sat down at her Grandma's table. "Grandma what is going on with this house?" She mumbled aloud. "Did you and Granddad ever discover what this thing is that plagues your home?" She held her head. "If you knew, why didn't you tell me about it?" She felt so tired, but braced herself for the day ahead.

"Cassie, it's time to get up, baby." She pulled herself from the dining table and scooted over to the stairs. "Cassie, are you up?" She could feel the panic swelling in her chest. Just as she started to track up the stairs, Cassie came out as Granddad would say "bright eyed and bushy tailed." Leigh smiled; relieved Cassie's night had gone well. "Look at you. Did you sleep well?"

"Yes, I did. Not one disturbance." She bounced past Leigh and into the kitchen for her morning Cheerios. Leigh followed, not so bouncy. She had to laugh at herself. She was getting old. She wanted a moment with Cassie to persuade her not to tell Josh about their reasons for moving back to Louisville. She sat across from her daughter with her favorite coffee cup refilled. "Cassie, I need to discuss something with you."

Cassie replaced her spoon of Cheerios in the bowl and looked at her mom. "Mom, I am telling Josh about this." She stared her mother down. "I'm sorry, but I will do everything in my power to keep us here." She softened her stare. "I don't want to leave not only Josh, but my friends, my best friend, Sarah, the animals, our family. Think about it Mom, these are the reasons you made us move in the first place."

Before Leigh could comment, Josh was at the front door. Not waiting for a reply, Cassie ran to open the door. Leigh couldn't help but notice the glow her daughter had when she was with Josh. Why was this happening? She was tired—physically and mentally. She grabbed her boots and slid them on. Mumbling again, "It feels horrible getting old." She pushed herself out the door and headed toward the barn. The more she walked, the more alive she felt; she loved the animals.

Josh and Cassie sat in silence while they rode down the highway. Josh was holding Cassie's hand tight as if he was sure Leigh was going to snatch her away today unless he kept her close. Cassie held his just as tight. Finally, Josh got up the strength to address the elephant sitting in the truck with them. "Cassie, why would your mom do this?" He took quick looks at Cassie while he drove down the curvy road. "Is the job she's going back to so much better than the farm?" As if talking to himself he affirmed, "I know she loves your farm."

Cassie stared at Josh so long that he began to feel uneasy about what she was going to tell him. He wanted to tell her to spit it out, but resisted. Cassie looked away and pretended the sight from the side window was interesting, but she gave herself away with the frown line. Josh had noticed that when she got aggravated about anything she had the cutest frown line next to her left eye.

He smiled; he was learning so much about this great girl, and now she was going to be taken away. It just couldn't happen; he would not allow it; there had to be something to stop this move.

He tried to remain patient while Cassie mustered up enough courage to continue. Finally, she blurted out, "Josh, what I am going to tell you right now is going to be hard for you to believe." Her eyes darted around the room, anywhere except looking in Josh's. She didn't want to see the disbelief once he heard the real reason they were leaving. "You are going to have to believe each and every story I tell you actually occurred. The incidents are not from an over-active imagination." She stopped to give him time to react. He just watched her face as he waited for the next shoe to fall.

"Since Mom and I moved in the house … things … weird things have been happening." She looked at him for feedback but only found a face in complete concentration on each word she said. If the discussion hadn't been so serious, she would have giggled. He was unbelievably cute. She began again. "I have experienced things from the moment we first moved in and now it is happening with my mom and with both of us together."

"What do you mean weird things are happening?" Josh was soaking up the information like a sponge. He wanted to know everything, and then he could help solve the problem.

Cassie gave him one more glance before dropping her eyes and spoke. "You remember the first day we went four-wheeling?" Josh nodded, wanting her to continue.

"Remember the lady that came to visit my mom on the porch as we left and I commented that I was glad she wasn't alone all day?"

Josh was trying to remember, but couldn't think of anything that was happening that morning except for how cute this new neighbor was. He shook his head that he didn't remember. "Tell me what happened." Concern washed over his face, "Is there something I did that morning that made your mom not happy with me?"

Cassie snapped her blue eyes back to Josh's face. "No ... no she likes you." Cassie quickly came back to the topic of the lady, "Well you see, there actually wasn't a lady standing with my mom. She told me she hadn't been around anyone all day long." She looked into Josh's face. He was trying so hard to comprehend what she was saying. "I saw this woman's clothes, even the smile on her face as she waved bye to me."

Josh started, "Cassie, I'm sure there is a logical explanation—"

Cassie cut him off, "No, there isn't!" She nervously played with her hair. "We have both seen her in the house at different times since we have been living there." She raised her hand when she saw Josh getting the courage to argue her down about the lady; she needed to get the whole story out there while she was on a roll.

"There are other things, once pillows went flinging across the room, and I felt something heavy sitting on my chest. Another time, I felt someone's breathing on my neck yet there was no one around. Mom and I have both heard loud, jump-out-of-your-skin, noises. The last time something occurred, Mom finally acknowledged that something was going on in the house."

"The other night there was a noise that sounded as if a train had hit the side of the kitchen. When we ran to the kitchen, the cabinet drawers and all the contents were scattered all over the floor."

Cassie stole a glance at Josh. She struggled to make him understand the seriousness of the situation. "Not one drawer, but each and every one of them lay scattered on the floor. Mom has admitted that there's eerie things happening and she is scared for me. That's why we are leaving Grandma and Granddad's farm."

Finished, she cast her eyes back toward Josh. Would he believe her or would he laugh? She searched his face for answers. She found him looking very sternly at her face.

"Why have you waited to tell me this until now Cassie? Why would you try to deal with this alone?" He didn't even question her to see if he could find a reason not to believe her. She was falling for this boy. She reached over and gave him a kiss. She didn't care that he was driving; she could not resist. They smiled at each other.

She dragged herself back to the situation at hand and answered. "I don't know. Maybe I didn't say anything for the same reason that Mom asked me not to say anything. I was afraid you wouldn't believe me or think I was crazy."

Josh's brain was in problem-solving mode. "There has to be a reason these things are occurring. Wonder if your great-grandparents experienced any of these things?"

"Why would Granddad and Grandma give us their house without telling us what was happening? I don't believe they knew."

"Okay, we have to find out the history of the house. That will tell us why things are happening at least." Josh felt that if he had something to work with, he could solve the mystery. He refused to lose this battle. "Now that I know what is truly motivating your mom, we can work on changing her mind."

He pulled into the school parking lot and pulled Cassie to him. "I refuse to allow you to leave." And for the moment, Cassie believed him. She felt safe and loved in his arms. He reached down to pull her chin up to face him and gave her the most gentle and loving kiss she had ever known. She felt her breath leave. She felt she was moving through space and time, and she didn't want to come back to reality.

His face was flushed. His voice was course and rough. "We have to go to class." They disentangled themselves and stepped out of the Chevy and walked up the walkway greeting all their friends that were lounging around before classes began.

The day passed without incident. Leigh had lost interest in remodeling the house and spent the day trying to gain back the sleep she had lost the night before. She kept waiting for something to occur, but the house was quiet. It was as if it knew she had forced them to move away, and now it could stop. She pulled herself from the couch, and scooted to the kitchen to pour more coffee.

She had phone calls from Anita and several from Mark. She knew he was going to tell her about the contracts he had for the planting of the fields. Leigh couldn't face telling him there would be no need for contracts because she and Cassie were leaving. Her heart was so heavy that she refused to face Mark with this gloom hovering over her shoulders. She'd wait until tomorrow.

Her thoughts drifted to her daughter. She had seen the look of determination on Cassie's face when she had discussed the need to be quiet about the house. Leigh didn't want the whole community laughing at the silly city girls for allowing their girly fears to get the best of them. She would laugh herself had she not witnessed the incidents.

She came to the conclusion that worrying about Cassie telling wasn't going to help; she was going to tell Josh everything. Leigh was still tired, and there was nothing she could do about the situation. She turned over on the couch and drifted off to sleep for the third or fourth time today.

Fifteen

Leigh rolled over to take a look at the television that had kept her company all day; not one unexplained turning on or turning off on its own all day. Oh my goodness, "Days of Our Lives" was on, that meant it was after three in the afternoon, and she had lain on the couch in her misery the whole day. Cassie would be home soon, and she hadn't accomplished anything. Then again, what did she need to be doing? They were leaving.

She needed to get food ready for the kids, she better get busy. She made herself jump up and felt her legs go weak. She had really been lying a long time; her legs were ready to buckle. She moved slowly into the kitchen and began pulling boxes for dinner. She stared at the half remodeled room. It would have been her best effort yet. She'd have to take the tiles back to the store. She'd already gotten the walls painted. As she admired the paint color she'd chosen, she stopped frozen in her spot. On the back wall there was a deep indented paint message. "Mine" was plainly written in darker paint over the sunny yellow she had chosen. She stood staring in a daze at the back wall.

That's how Josh and Cassie found her. Josh didn't see anything at first, just Leigh motionless. She snapped back into human mode once she saw and heard the kids. "Hey, guys how was school?" She had a genuine smile for the both of them. She didn't want to be the evil mom. She knew the strength of their connection right now and she could only hope that with the move Cassie and Josh would find others they felt as strongly about. She laughed at herself. Who was she kidding—she too had left her one true love to move away to the big city and she was still fighting the pull of that connection.

Cassie hadn't noticed. "It was a good day. I feel as if I

have been here my whole life. I belong here." She said the last statement while piercing her mother with her eyes. Josh, on the other hand, had found what Leigh was looking at and also saw her shake her head slightly. She didn't want to frighten Cassie. Josh decided to go along with Leigh this time. He had goose bumps running up and down his body. He couldn't believe what he was seeing. Maybe Leigh had written it herself. But why would she write notes on the wall? To scare them into agreeing this was for the best? It wasn't for the best, and he was going to make sure of that. He had to know . . . "Been painting today, Mrs. Ward?"

Leigh knew what he was doing, and she didn't mind. She herded them out of the kitchen as she brought snacks to the dining room. "No, I have taken it easy all day long today." She chirped.

Josh got the message loud and clear. He wasn't going to lie to himself; he was more than a little freaked out by what he had witnessed. He would have to act fast if he had any chance of keeping Cassie here with him. Although, he understood Leigh's protective instinct now that he'd seen the message on the wall literally spelled out for them. He intended to find out what was going on with this house. But for the moment, he and Cassie were enjoying being together, and he was going to make sure they enjoyed this evening without stressing about their future.

He took half of the plate of breadsticks leaving Cassie the other and ate most of his before Cassie could get started. She offered him half of what she had. He smiled as he scooped several from her plate explaining, "Lunch was horrible today." He looked up and smiled at both daughter and mother. They giggled while he dug in again. They gave up and laughed as he joined in with the laughter, making the situation funnier by exaggerating the dipping of bread into the sauce. He gave Cassie a sideways glance as he stuffed more bread into his mouth.

Once they finished, Cassie led him outside, and they walked hand in hand to the barn to feed the animals. Leigh looked out the window and smiled. She had never seen her daughter as happy as she was when Josh was around. When Anita and she were in high school, they never dreamed they would have children that would be so close. She thought about calling Anita to tell her about her thoughts and decided she couldn't right now. Anita was too close; she would hear the worry in her voice if she talked with her on the phone. If Anita could help her, she would have called her first thing. But, this situation was something that no one could help with, and she didn't want to drag Anita into the mess. No, this was one time she was alone, and she was the one that had to make the tough decision, even if it meant making her daughter miserable. She would be better miserable than in danger.

She hurried to the kitchen, grabbed the paint roller and painted over the word left on the wall. She felt the familiar shivers begin, but she was so angry that she wouldn't allow it to make her afraid. She wanted to confront and conquer this thing in her house. She painted harder and faster feeling that her anger and frustration could be deleted from the energy she was using to cover the message. After she had finished, she hesitated. She kept thinking that at any moment, something would happen. She waited, but there was no retaliation.

Finally, she dragged herself back to her couch and found her spot that she had buried herself in all day. She couldn't remember a time she was this depressed. She fluctuated from depression to anger to hurt to disappointment.

She was still lying in the silence of the room when the kids came bursting in the door giggling about something that the cows had done. They were so happy; it made her even more depressed. Cassie asked her mom if she could go over to Josh's to help him with his chores and Leigh agreed. "Tell your mom I said hi, will you?"

"I will," Josh agreed. Cassie hugged her mother and followed Josh out of the house. Leigh pushed herself off the couch and watched out the window as the two climbed in the Chevy.

Once again, she found herself alone. She felt

loneliness envelop her. It was hard to have only one's self to discuss your problems. She sighed and slid back to the couch and found her spot once again and lay down contemplating what to do first.

Josh and Cassie went quickly to the barn and worked as swiftly as they could, getting the animals comfortable for the night. Once they finished, they walked down the path that led to Josh's grandmother's house. The first thing they needed was information about the house, and Josh knew his grandmother was one of the smartest people he had ever known. She would give them sound advice on what they should do to make Leigh change her mind. When they reached the front door, Josh gave it three long knocks and opened. He called, "Mammy?"

They heard Mammy coming from the kitchen. Her breath was labored, and Cassie worried she wouldn't make it into the living room to meet them. She walked with the help of a walker into the living room smiling. "Josh, I love hearing that beautiful voice. Now who is this lovely thing you have brought for me to see?"

Josh grinned, "Mammy, this is Leigh Howard's daughter, Cassie. They have moved back to Salyersville and are living on the Howard Farm, in Leigh's grandparents' house."

Mammy frowned, "No, I didn't know they had moved in the house." She leaned into Cassie. "How do you like this place young lady?"

Cassie moved closer to the old lady and pronounced, "I feel that I have come home. I love living on the farm with all the animals."

Josh cleared his throat, "Mammy, we have something we need to talk to you about. It's going to sound funny, but we need to know."

The elderly woman made herself comfortable in her favorite chair and sat back to listen to the plight of Josh and Cassie. It was obvious that she was delighted someone was in need of her advice. "Spit it out, I'm ready."

Josh sat next to Cassie, giving her an encouraging look and took a deep breath. "Cassie and her mother have been experiencing some strange things over at the Howard house, Mammy. We thought you could help us with the history surrounding the house so we can figure out what to do about it." He paused long enough to look at his grandmother. "Can you help us? Do you know of anything that has been strange about the house throughout the years?"

Mammy got a faraway look before beginning to tell her story. "I have heard things about that house since I was a girl. The house was new when I first heard of strange goings-on. When I was a girl, the story was that the owner was a man named Cooper. He married Margret Ann Howard. I was told she was the prettiest wife on the creek. He actually built that house for her. It was a grand house back in those days." Mammy shrugged her frail shoulders, "Still is."

Cassie interrupted, "So, I don't understand what was strange. It sounds romantic to me."

Mammy's beady black eyes pierced Cassie's face. She smiled at the girl and then settled back into her story. "Oh, it was romantic until the pretty wife turned up missing. The husband said she had took sick and died. There wasn't a funeral or anything. Said he was too hurt, but there were rumors."

Josh was beginning to perk up, "What were the rumors, Mammy?"

"Well, it was said that Cooper's wife was pretty, and all the creek's men were in love with her. All the neighbors said the husband was so jealous that he did something to cause Margret Ann's demise. No one could prove it, so he got clean away with killing her. He had money and power so no one questioned him too much."

Cassie looked at Josh, "Could that be the lady that keeps visiting us? But why?" She turned toward Mammy. "Did you say her last name was Howard?" Mammy nodded. "Could she have been related to us? We are Howard's." Cassie reasoned to herself, forgetting the others in the room.

Mammy nodded once again. "It is possible that she

was related to your Granddad. I never heard anyone say. From what I remember about her, she came from a neighboring county –Morgan County, I think."

"Maybe she knows we are her relatives and she wants to tell us something. She might just want to tell someone why she was killed. Maybe she doesn't want to hurt anyone." She looked at Josh, searching for confirmation of her theory. He was deep in thought.

They didn't realize that Mammy wasn't finished with the story until she began again, "Once the wife was gone, he sold out to a woman and her two daughters. Everyone said he couldn't stand to live in the house where he had killed his love. Guilt must have been getting the best of him."

Josh began, "Mammy, this has been very helpful—."

Mammy interrupted him, "I'm not finished."

Josh stopped and smiled. "Sorry, Mammy."

Mammy continued, "Now those women that bought the house was friendly enough, but one day my friend, Madge, had walked to the grocery store and had her arms full of groceries. At that time, everyone walked to the country store to get groceries. So, Madge had gone after her groceries, and as she passed the house the old woman that lived there asked her to come in and rest for a while before she went on home. Madge was so tired that she took her up on it and went inside to cool down. As they sat talking, the old woman called for her daughters to come into the sitting room. Then all three put one of their hands on the surface top of a small table, and Madge watched as the three chanted, "Rise—Table—Rise." over and over. With one hand of each woman resting on top of the table, Madge watched as the table rose from the floor. Madge told me herself that the table came off the floor at least five inches. She said the woman told her they were practicing witches. Scared her to death!" Mammy chuckled, "She never got so tired that she had to rest at that house ever again."

Mammy got a longing look that went back into the past, "I truly miss my friend, Madge. We were the best of friends. Next to your Grandpa, Madge was the closest person to me." Mammy smiled a smile that was meant for her and her memories. She made her way back from the past to the present and shook her head with a soft sigh, "That woman and her girls didn't stay too long. They sold out to your granddad, young lady. Howard's have lived there ever since."

Cassie had to know, "Mammy, did you ever hear of any strange things happening while my great-grandparents lived in the house?"

Mammy frowned creasing her wrinkled face. "I heard Lizzy say once that just before she lost one of the twins, she heard a loud knock on the side of the house, like someone threw a large rock against the house." Mammy rubbed her face in an attempt to remember important details from the past. "I remember her telling that she'd heard something before your Uncle Tom had his wreck that took his arm."

Cassie swallowed, "Mammy, do you know if Granddad and Grandma were scared of the house?" She had to know if her great-grandparents knew about the house. But, if they did, why didn't they tell her mom about it?

Mammy shook her head, "No, they knew there were things going on in the house, but they were willing to live with them, so long as they didn't hurt them. They must have made peace with it because they lived in that house a long time."

Josh moved in closer to Mammy, "Is there anything else you can think of, Mammy?" He searched her face for any remaining information she hadn't spoken of yet. But he didn't find anything.

Mammy shook her head, "Nothing more I can think of at the moment. I'll try to think some more and you two come back for a visit, and we'll talk some more."

Josh cackled, "You're good, Mammy. You'll do anything for company."

Mammy laughed with him, "I'll even make you a red velvet cake."

Josh winked at Cassie, "Throw in a bowl of your home

canned peaches, and you have a deal."

"It's a deal. You come too, young lady."

Cassie quickly agreed to come back with Josh. Mammy remarked mostly to herself, "What a cute couple they make."

Josh and Cassie grinned at each other and hugged Mammy before bidding her goodbye. As they started for the door, Josh turned back to his grandmother, "Mammy, I forgot to ask you not to mention this to anyone. Cassie's mom, Leigh, doesn't want anyone to know what's going on with the house."

Mammy pulled her wrinkled arthritic finger to her lips, "Mums the word."

"Thanks, Mammy, you have helped a lot. Now all we have to do is figure out how to get past the stuff happening in the house so Cassie can stay in Salyersville."

Mammy smiled, "So young to love so strong." She reached out for the two to come back to her. They obeyed, and she hugged them both at once. "Don't let anything get in the way of true love." She raked her wrinkled hand across both their faces. She then pushed them toward the door. "Go enjoy the day you two. Just come visit me soon." They agreed and left with smiles pasted on their faces.

They were both deep in thought as they made their way back to Josh's house. Once they made it back, they climbed into the truck and headed back to Cassie's. They were silent; trying to decipher the information Mammy had given them. They had a lot to think about, but neither knew what to do with the information they had discovered. The truck pulled in front of Cassie's house, and Josh reached over to pull Cassie close. "I have had a great day, Cassie." He didn't give her time to reply. He pulled his lips over hers and kissed her with all the love and tenderness his heart was feeling. Cassie returned his kiss with her own heart. Neither Josh nor Cassie dared to approach the thought that plagued their thoughts. What would they do if Leigh couldn't be persuaded to stay in Salyersville?

Sixteen

The next day started their weekend. Josh and Cassie had made plans to meet their friends on the four-wheeler trail for the Saturday ride. Cassie got up early to help with the chores in the barn and reminded her mom she was going four-wheeling with Josh. Leigh smiled a smile that didn't reach her eyes and told Cassie to have fun with her friends. Cassie was preoccupied but not to the point that she didn't notice the sadness of her mother. She had seen her mom like this only one other time and that was when her dad had left and they were getting a divorce.

Cassie realized the plan to move back to Louisville was hurting her mom as much as it was hurting her. Why couldn't they just stay? It had been days since she had heard or seen anything from the house. Maybe whatever was causing these things to happen was gone.

She looked at her mom and was torn with the sadness of her mother and the day she had planned with Josh. She couldn't bear her mom being alone in the house all day. As bad as she hated to give up time with Josh she found herself offering, "Mom, why don't I send Josh with his friends and you and I spend the day together? Let's have a mother-daughter day. What do you say, is it a date?"

Leigh gave Cassie a weak smile and refused. "No, I have plans to visit Anita today. Although, it's so sweet of you to offer to give up your day with Josh, just to spend time with your old mom. I am touched. Thank you, my beautiful daughter."

Cassie watched as Leigh's slumped shoulders made their way back across the road to the house. Cassie was worried about her mother. She wasn't sure if there was anything she could do to help her through this and that was the hardest thing to deal with. She was still standing in the barn when she saw Josh's truck pull up in front of the house.

Her face beamed in spite of herself. Josh…he was so good in her life. She refused to move away. But Cassie knew her mother; there was no stopping her once she made her mind up about something. Maybe Josh's mom could persuade her to change her mind. She had always been someone Mom listened to when she needed advice.

She ran across the road to meet Josh on the porch. "Hey, good looking. How about taking a girl for a ride on that contraption?" She gave it her best country accent, which was awful. They both laughed at her attempt.

Josh then replied using his own country drawl, "Yes, ma'am. Anytime you feel like a ride, you just hop on Myrtle here, and we'll take us a spin." His was much better than Cassie's, yet Cassie was giggling just the same. As Cassie opened the door to go inside, Josh caught her by the arm and pulled her to him so that he could whisper, "good morning, beautiful," while kissing her and as their lips parted he pushed her inside the house.

She giggled once again and whispered back, "Good morning to you, handsome." As they entered the living room, Cassie's high spirits fell. She saw her mom sitting on the couch with her coffee mug resting on her lap. Leigh had a smile pasted on her face and pretended to be busy flipping through the channels on the television as they entered.

Cassie and Josh sat down with Leigh for a moment to discuss their plans for the day. Leigh told them to be safe and to have fun. Cassie found herself offering again to postpone the outing and spend the day with her mom. She watched Josh's face, expecting him to show anger or disappointment at her suggestion, but she only saw concern mirrored on his face. He had seen her mother's sadness, just as she had. If it was obvious even to Josh, they had to do something. "Mom, you are going over to Anita's, right? I don't want you spending the day alone, not on a Saturday."

Leigh raised her mug to take a sip and nodded. "Yes, I am going to visit with my friend, Anita. I am going to be just fine. I am old enough to find things to entertain myself. You two go have fun. Anita and I will have just as much fun as the two of you; we always do." She forced a bright smile again and waved them out the door. They all laughed, and she followed them out onto the porch and watched as they drove away. Just as before, Cassie turned and waved bye to her mother. Leigh wondered what Cassie saw today when she looked back at the porch. Did she see only Leigh standing on the porch or was the lady in white or black or whatever she felt like that day, standing beside her?

Leigh felt a chill although the morning was already warm and sunny. She made her way back into the house and made a quick call to Anita. She might as well break the news to her good friend. She knew the day would be hard. Anita wouldn't allow her to give up so easily.

Cassie's heart had been pounding as she made herself turn to wave at her mother. She was so afraid of what she would see standing on the porch. This time she only saw her mother standing alone. She was worried. Her mother needed friends. Cassie decided that she would call Uncle Ray and Aunt Betty to come over to visit. They had been at the house long enough now that they could have people over for dinner. Besides, it would only be Uncle Ray and Aunt Betty, it would do Mom good. Besides, she wanted to quiz Uncle Ray about the former resident of Howard farm ... Margret Ann Howard.

Once she had a plan of action, she moved closer to Josh and squeezed tighter. She turned her face to the wind, and for a fleeting moment she didn't think of anything or anyone except for the exhilarating wind on her face. Before long they stopped at the familiar tree by the creek and waited for the others to join them.

This time they didn't spend all their time getting to know each other. They spent most of the time kissing and staring into each other's eyes. They were locked together in an embrace when they heard the roar of another four-wheeler coming across the hill. Josh hesitantly moved just a few inches away but kept his hand nestled with Cassie's. She welcomed the feel of his large hand holding hers, as if he was protecting her from all that was bad around them.

Jake squawked, "Look at the love birds. You two look like you have made up and are back on track." Sarah jumped off the four-wheeler giving him an elbow in the side. She gave Cassie a genuinely pleased smile and Cassie smiled back with just as much pleasure. Sarah was a good friend. Hadn't she stuck with her even though she and Josh were longtime friends? Sarah had made sure that Cassie knew that she could depend on her friendship during the Kari escapade.

They all sat down under the tree to wait for the others. Cassie's thoughts quickly moved to the day she had been under the tree and had felt the breath on her neck. The goose bumps begin to surface again as she snuggled closer to Josh. He automatically curved his arm around her, pulling her closer. Sarah's smile, as she watched the two of them together, said it all. Cassie had forgotten that, only weeks ago, she and Josh were just friends, and a few days before that, they had been fighting. It seemed like a lifetime ago.

Since the ordeal with the house, she hadn't had time to think of Kari. She made a mental note to ask Josh about the situation once they were alone. After lounging on the moss carpet under the tree, listening to the stream of water moving over the rocks they heard the roar of the remaining four-wheelers. Cassie smiled as she watched the same boys that had made her jaw drop on the drive to the Creek. Never in a million years had she believed these hunks would be her friends. If Jessica and Megan could see her now, they would be so jealous. She would take pictures of the group today and send it to the girls to gawk at tonight. She laughed at herself; she still wanted to brag about her good fortune, even if her friends back in Louisville thought she was sent away to prison. Hadn't she felt the same way when she first came here? Now all she wanted was to stay put.

They all climbed on their four-wheelers, and headed up the hill. Cassie felt free as a bird, free of all the turmoil at home. She would be like Scarlet O'Hara, she would think about it tomorrow.

Josh, on the other hand, was thinking about it now. He had seen how sad Leigh had looked this morning. He didn't want her to be sad, but maybe they could work it to help persuade her to stay at Howard Farm. The only person he knew that could help was his mother. He pretended he had to use the bathroom and moved away from the group. He pulled out his cell phone hoping he had service. He was lucky; his mom's phone was ringing.

"Hello."

"Hello, Mom?"

Anita's frightened reply came back, "Josh, are you alright? What is wrong? Are you kids okay? Where are you? I'm coming."

Josh had to laugh at his mother. She was always ready to defend and protect. "Mom, nothing is wrong. Everyone is fine. We're having a good time."

Anita's voice turned from fright to anger, "So, why are you calling to scare me, son?" Then her voice changed to the loving mother, "Okay, what's up? I know you didn't just call me because you love me."

Josh had to play along for a moment, "But, I do love you, Mommy." He laughed when he heard her snicker in the phone. "Okay, I have an ulterior motive."

Anita burst into the phone, "I knew it."

Josh hesitated and decided it was time to get serious. "I need your help, Mom."

"That is what I'm here for, Josh. What can your old mom do for you? Just ask."

"Cassie and I are worried about Leigh. She seems very sad. Since she has decided to move back to Louisville—."

Anita screamed into the phone, "MOVE BACK TO LOUISVILLE? SHE IS NOT MOVING BACK TO LOUISVILLE!" Gaining composure she continued, "Why do you think that she is moving back to Louisville?"

Josh knew he had divulged more than he should have. He tried to smooth out the mistake. "Mom, I am sure she is going to tell you about it today when she sees you. You two just haven't been together yet. I only know because of

Cassie. Anyway, Mom, Cassie and I need your help in persuading Leigh to stay here in Salyersville."

Anita, much calmer, wondered aloud, "What would make her even think about moving back to that city again? I know she is happy here."

Josh had to hurry, "Mom, please, will you talk with her for us. Please persuade her that this is the best place for Cassie and her?"

"I'm on it, Son. It will be my priority for the day."

Josh knew he had taken too long on the phone, "I got to go Mom, Thank you. I love you."

Anita smiled at the phone, "Yeah, yeah, yeah, I love you too," Then she added, "With all my heart."

Josh smiled back at his phone and put it back into his pocket while running back to the four-wheelers. Jake shouted out, "I thought we were going to have to leave you here in this thicket to walk back." Several of the boys laughed while Josh ran to join them.

He settled himself on his four-wheeler and pulled Cassie's arms tight around his waist, ready to climb the next hill. He smiled to himself. His mom was on the job. She wouldn't allow Leigh to ruin their lives. His mom took no prisoners, and for once he was glad. He had been on the other end of her relentless digging for the truth. Leigh didn't have a chance.

Cassie and Josh dismissed their anxiety over their situation for the day and just enjoyed themselves. As always Cassie loved the feel of the wind on her face and the comfortable easy feeling she had when she sat behind Josh. She felt his muscles move as he compensated for her on the back of the four-wheeler. He was her protector, and she loved it. Her face felt sore from the wind, and the constant smile she couldn't stop. Life was so good living in Salyersville and next door to Josh.

They stopped for lunch, and everyone was in a good mood. Cassie guessed they were happy to see their longtime friend happy. And she felt they were genuinely happy she was there. She was a part of this group, and she was thrilled to have them as her best friends. She and

Sarah were becoming closer each day. For a fleeting moment, she allowed her mind to think about how devastated she would be if she had to leave her new best friend. It hurt her to her core, almost as much as when she thought about leaving Josh. She shook her head and made herself focus on the corny joke Jake was telling. Everyone was laughing at the way he was telling it, not the joke itself. She loved being with these people. She joined in with the laughter and without any effort she had forgotten her troubles and found it easy to enjoy the day.

Seventeen

Anita couldn't believe that Josh had the correct information. She knew that Leigh was happy to be back in town. What could have happened in the short length of time since she had last talked with her? Although, she mused, she had been calling Leigh for the past few days without any response. Was Leigh avoiding her? She did the same thing when they were in high school. If something happened, Leigh always holed up in her bedroom; not allowing anyone to see her until she could solve the problem or at least come to terms with it. Well, this time avoidance was not going to work.

She picked up her phone and pushed in Leigh's number. The phone rang several times and then she heard Leigh's recorded voice instructing her to leave a message. She waited until the beep and barked, "Leigh, I know you're home, and I am on my way to your house. Do not leave…do not hide. You can't get away from me, my friend."

She put her phone down and grabbed her keys. As she pulled into the driveway, she saw the red Explorer parked out front. So, Leigh was home. Anita readied herself for battle; she knows I won't give up. She walked to the door and knocked. She waited and knocked again while mumbling, "If she doesn't answer this door, I'll—." The door sprang open, and there stood a disheveled Leigh.

Anita wasn't ready for what happened next. Leigh flung herself into Anita's arms and sobbed. Anita's fight disappeared while her compassion and love for her friend overwhelmed her. She moved Leigh into the house and closed the door. The two sat down on the couch, and Anita listened as Leigh spilled the whole unbelievable story.

Every once in a while Leigh would pause to study Anita to see if she was taking her seriously. Anita's face showed only love and concern.

Once Leigh had spilled everything, including her reservoir of tears, she stopped and sat back in her seat while nervously playing with the tissue Anita had given her. It was silent for what seemed like hours. Leigh was giving Anita time to digest what she had told her. She hadn't held anything back. As they sat in silence, Leigh was feeling guilty for dumping the whole mess on her friend, but she knew Anita wouldn't stop until she had all the information.

Just having her best friend beside her made her feel better. Leigh felt her tense body begin to relax while waiting for Anita to soak up all she had unloaded on her. Just knowing that even if her friend couldn't come up with a solution to this horrific situation, Anita would stand by her and she had listened. Leigh looked at her friend and offered an apology. "Sorry to dump all that on you."

Anita believed her story. She didn't think Leigh was being delusional about what was occurring with the house. "Okay, now that we have that out of the way, let's break this down so we can figure out what and why this is happening. Let's see if we can find any common factors with each manifestation or event."

Anita was already pulling paper from Granddad's side table to chart out the happenings. As she drew her web, she looked up to find her friend smiling through a new stream of tears. Leigh sobbed, "You are the best friend I ever could have asked for, Anita Johnson. Thank you, for just being you."

Anita put down her pencil and gave her friend a hug. "Through thick and thin, remember? What else would I be doing when my friend needs my expert meddling?" And since Anita had been known her whole life as the "fixer" they both laughed.

Throughout the day, Leigh noticed Anita never asked her to stay in the house. She was afraid to ask her friend what she thought about her moving back to Louisville. She thought she might leave that on the shelf until later. Leigh knew Anita, and she had no doubts that she would get back to that subject. Leigh braced herself. She had to think of Cassie and not what she wanted. She had to keep her daughter safe.

She watched in silence as Anita worked on her chart of events. Leigh sighed, if only the house had worked out for them, her best friend's child and her child might have made a life together.

Yes, they were both very young to feel this strongly about each other. But, look at her; she had found her true love when she wasn't any older than Cassie. She had given him up to pursue her career. She sighed and allowed the sadness to show its ugly self for only a moment. She thought about her life now and what it could have been if she had stayed in Salyersville with Mark. She didn't want this feeling of loss for Cassie. She and Josh were so happy right now. She sighed again. Anita pulled her eyes from the paper long enough to chide her friend. "Bored, are you? This ghost hunting not exciting enough for you?" They both laughed, and Anita got back to business. She was like a hound dog before the hunt.

They were still charting the strange events at the farm when they heard the four-wheeler park outside. In a few moments, Cassie and Josh burst into the room. Their faces were full of life. Josh looked at his mother, "Mom, are you still here?" His face gave away his discomfort. He wasn't sure how Cassie and Leigh would take his involving his mother. He didn't have to wait long to find out that the two friends were glad the situation was out in the open. His mom had been very strategic about his involvement in her learning of the problem. He hugged his mom and whispered in her ear a quick "thank you."

She squeezed him tighter and whispered back, "No, no, thank you for telling me, my son." Both pairs of eyes that were identical had a glint of sparkle to them as they came back to the others in the room.

After discussing the familiar: how their day was; what they had done today; gossip since they had started the new school year; the two teens said their goodbyes and used the excuse of taking care of chores as their getaway plan.

The routine of Josh helping Cassie and then Cassie helping Josh with their barn chores was one of Cassie's favorite times of the day. She had the best her world could offer; the animals and Josh. She felt as if she could float away if Josh didn't have her hand to keep her anchored.

The two mothers, peeping out the window, watched as their offspring walked toward the barn hand in hand. Leigh spoke first, "They look happy, Anita."

Knowing the reaction she would get from her friend, Anita responded, "Just think about it, some day we might be grandmas together." She got the reaction she was looking for; Leigh's eyes went wide, and her mouth dropped open.

"Anita, they are entirely too young to be thinking like that. We have to allow them to make their own lives." Anita burst out laughing.

"Got you." She laughed. Leigh picked up the large pillow resting on the couch and flung it at Anita. They both laughed and settled back to the window to watch their precious children. "Are we spying on our children?" Asked Anita.

"Yes," was all Leigh could manage before she bent over laughing once again. They moved away from the window and sat just chatting for a moment before Anita announced it was time for her to go, she had to do the evening chores. Leigh nodded as she hugged her friend one last time.

"Thank you for showing up on my doorstep today. You are the best friend a girl could ever have."

Anita, her eyes dancing, quipped, "I know." She swept up the chart and told Leigh bye one last time and then bounced out to her Rover. Leigh was alone once again. She plopped down on the couch as she felt the familiar loneliness. But this time she was comforted with knowing she wasn't alone in this mess. Her best friend would be by her side through it all.

Eighteen

When Cassie returned to the house, she found her mother sitting on the couch, where she usually found her sitting lately. Cassie wrinkled her brow; she had never seen her mother so sad. She looked sick sitting on that same spot she had sat in every day for the past week. She had to think of something that would make her come to life again.

She had planned to shout out that she was going but decided to sit down with her mom for a moment. "Mom, are you feeling okay? Has anything happened with the house today?" Cassie had been happy since the house had remained quiet for a while. As she thought about this, she realized they had not had an incident since they had decided to leave. Oh, no. Was the house trying to get them to leave? She refused to believe this or at least not allow her mother to believe it. She kept her epiphany to herself.

Leigh looked lovingly at her daughter, "I see how happy you are, Cassie. Josh and you are both good kids, and you just go together. I don't want to destroy that; I really don't." She looked up at her daughter, and the all too familiar tears began to fall once again. Would she never get past this?

"Josh and I won't let anything come between us, Mom. I know you just want the best for me; I do." She saw Josh in the doorway, "We're going to make sure you feel safe and that you know staying here is the best thing for us."

Josh smiled and cleared his throat before he sauntered into the room. "I know my Mom is a handful, but I've never known her to leave a crowd crying." They all laughed. Anita was one person they all knew that would strive to fix anyone that was crying.

Leigh laughed through her tears, "Your mother is the best person I have ever known. And, she is my best friend, so don't you go talking about her."

Wow. Josh had snapped her mother back to her old self in seconds. How did he do that? Cassie marveled. "We better get going if we're going to get your livestock fed and put some hay out for the cattle. We still have to clean the horse stalls." Cassie rose from the couch, and stood beside Josh.

Leigh told her daughter and boyfriend goodbye and headed for the kitchen for some popcorn to snack on while watching the new "Big Brother" episode on the television. She was in a much better mood tonight since her best friend had spent the day with her. She smiled when she thought of Anita stooped over those charts all day, determined to solve the mystery. She had missed seeing her old friend when she lived in Louisville all those years. If she were to be honest, she would have to admit that she had missed Mark too. If her parents had been alive, she was positive she would have stayed in Salyersville.

At the time, she couldn't survive staying on Lick Creek where everywhere she turned she could see remnants of her mother and father's life. After the accident, she just wanted to start a new life that wouldn't remind her of her parents. She had started fresh and thought she was happy with Cassie's dad for many years. She thought she could have been fine with the way things were if Jack had not been the one asking for a divorce. The protective wall she'd pulled around her and her family began tumbling down, leaving her stronger to push through and live life.

She found living back in the world of her young life the easiest thing she had attempted since she was a young woman driving away from this very house and her grandparents. She shook her head to clear the memories and focused on the contestants arguing on "Big Brother."

Her phone rang, and as she had done all week, she allowed it to ring without answering. Then, she heard Mark leaving a message. "Leigh, I've been trying to contact you all week and frankly, I'm getting more than a little worried. I'm on my way over to see you. I hope you receive this before I get there just so you won't be surprised, but I need to see you."

Leigh jumped off the couch and popcorn went flying like a hailstorm all over the furniture and floor. She raced to the bathroom to apply some makeup and comb her hair. Just as she started to brush her teeth the doorbell rang. For a moment, she weighed the consequences of not answering. She decided that wasn't a good idea since Mark had already seen her car parked in the driveway. She finished brushing and rinsed. She flew out of the bathroom and ran to the living room where she was reminded of the popcorn episode. She squeezed her eyes shut, walked past the mess, opened the door and smiled.

"Mark, how are you?"

Mark studied her face, "What is going on, Leigh? I know I'm supposed to keep my distance, but you are scaring me. Are you going to let me in this house?"

Leigh hesitated, "Mark, it's not a good time right now."

"Do you have company in there?" He did not flinch. She couldn't allow him to be angry because of another man in her house.

"Oh, all right. Come on in and see the mess, see if I care." She made a dramatic sweep of her hand as Mark made his way into the house. Once he saw what had happened to the living room, he laughed uncontrollably.

Leigh just looked on trying to keep a straight face while Mark snickered at the sight of her popcorn covered living room. Finally, Mark gained control and rubbed the tears from his eyes. "Okay, this is funny, but this isn't what has been keeping you from signing the leases for the fields. Those contracts are way over due, Leigh. This isn't like you. What's going on?"

He saw the look of despair on her face. In a much kinder voice, Mark asked, "Leigh, what has happened? What can I do to help you?" His love for this woman was so obvious at this moment, but he didn't care that he'd slipped and let his guard down. Leigh turned to face this kind man that she had loved since the days of her youth. Without speaking, they both knew the love that they had when they were young still lived. Mark grabbed her with gentle hands and kissed her with all the love he had pushed aside all these years. Leigh welcomed his love. She kissed him back as she hadn't kissed in years. They held each other without moving afraid this moment would disappear as dreams do.

As if by clockwork, Leigh heard Josh's truck pull up out front and by the time she and Mark had busied themselves with the contracts, Josh and Cassie were tumbling in the front door. Josh and Mark greeted each other and then Mark turned to greet Leigh's daughter. It was then that he felt the apprehension he was not used to feeling. No one he had ever known had made him feel the intimidation he was feeling because of this young girl. He was amazed.

Why was he allowing this teenager to make him feel inadequate? He knew the answer to this question. He wanted this girl to like him more than he wanted anything else in this world. If she didn't, the love of his life would be out of his reach once again. He had lost her once, and now he felt as if he could reach out and touch the life he'd always dreamed of having with Leigh.

He smiled at Cassie and reminded himself to tread lightly. He guardedly said, "Hello, Cassie, how are you doing?" He stopped his hand from picking at the pen that lay on the table in front of him.

Cassie smiled and replied, "Hello, Mark, I'm fine. How are you?" She noticed his nervousness and wondered what she and Josh had interrupted. Were her mother and Mark having a confrontation about work? Her mother looked flushed, yet she seemed in a good mood. Cassie was glad to see Leigh having a business meeting. That could only mean she wasn't absolutely set on moving. She seemed happy to be working with Mark. Josh had told her that Mark was a good fellow and that her mother could trust him as an honest business partner.

Mark interpreted Cassie's new friendliness as a good sign and became more at ease. He smiled at Leigh and began discussing the business he'd used as an excuse to come over. Leigh's face turned dark, and she tried to change the subject. How could she tell him she was leaving again; now, after what they had just experienced? She was very selfish with Mark, and he of all the people she knew didn't deserve to be treated this way. She tried to change the subject. "Let's have a seat and talk with the kids, shall we?" He looked a little confused but agreed. As they all sat down, Mark and Josh began talking about Josh's family. Leigh was thankful that Josh and Mark needed very little help in keeping the conversation going. Cassie and she sat watching the men comfortably discuss livestock, grain produced this year, and hay crops.

Cassie sat looking at the cozy little room. Why did they have to run from this home? She felt safe in this house, even with the incidents that had occurred. As she sat soaking in the coziness of the room and the company, her mind mused: there had been no problems with the house since they decided to leave. What was up with that?

Mark said he would discuss the contracts with Leigh in the morning. He shook Josh's hand and nodded to Cassie and left the cozy gathering. Josh took this as his hint that it was time to leave and allow the ladies to get some sleep. He wondered if Cassie had caught the looks Mark and Leigh were flashing each other. If she had seen it, she didn't seem concerned. He wasn't sure how Cassie would take it, but he thought it was perfect.

If Mark and Leigh became involved, Leigh would not leave. When he walked out to his truck, he walked with a spring in his step. For the first time, he was confident that Leigh could be persuaded to stay in Salyersville. He couldn't wait to tell his mother the good news.

Josh rushed in his house looking for his mom. "Mom, where are you? You are never going to believe what I have just witnessed."

Anita ran downstairs to find Josh in the kitchen stuffing his face with leftovers. "What happened?" She looked at her son intently. She couldn't stand being out of "the-know." Josh knew his mother's curiosity and so he lingered longer than he needed to until she punched his arm, "What happened? Is it good or is it something that will make me sad?"

Josh stole a look at her and then pretended to be concentrating on the barbecue wings. But his silence didn't last for long. He was too excited with what he had observed at the Howard's house. He quickly began telling her of his observation of Mark and Leigh. He looked at his mother for a reaction, but was surprised when he didn't get the reaction he expected. "Okay, what is the deal Mom? You don't look too surprised."

Anita grinned; it was her turn to hesitate and lead her son along. Josh stopped playing with the last wing and bellowed, "Mom. Out with it. What do you already know about this?"

Anita grinned. "Oh, I don't know anything about what's going on right now. All I can tell you is that Mark and Leigh were quite an item back in the day." She waited for Josh's reaction. He didn't disappoint.

"What? Does Cassie know any of this?"

Anita mumbled, "I don't think so. Or at least, Leigh hadn't told her." She glanced over at Josh, gave a loud sigh and blurted, "She told me she couldn't or wouldn't make Cassie any more uncomfortable than she already was from the move here." She slumped down on a stool and declared, "Now, you know everything I know."

Josh was still hopeful that this could be good news for them. "Do you think she might stay in Salyersville if she and Mark get back together? Especially if Cassie thought it was good for her mother?"

Anita pierced her son with her stare, "Josh, you cannot make Cassie agree with a relationship just because you want her to. It's not right. She will hate you in the end if anything bad happens."

Josh's face fell, "You're right, Mom, and I couldn't bear Cassie hating me." Josh plopped down on the stool next to his mom. "What should I do? I see a solution, but do I force it or let it play out? What if I do nothing and lose Cassie?"

Pointing her index finger in her son's face, Anita demanded, "YOU do nothing. I will do a little work on my own." Anita smiled. "I think it's time your dad and I had a welcome back to the neighborhood dinner for Leigh." She hesitated before continuing. "I think your father needs to discuss some business issues with Mark." Anita's face showed her satisfaction for her plan. "And, since Mark is a dear friend of all of ours, I'll have your father ask him to join us. What do you think?"

Josh reached across the bar and kissed his mother. "I think I love you, Mom." He ran upstairs and bounced into his room feeling better than he had in a long time. He looked over at the phone. He hadn't made a call to Kari since she had misled Cassie about them and he would not be making any calls, no matter what the consequences. He had to think about approaching Cassie with the truth about the calls to Kari. He'd do that as soon as this more pressing situation was fixed. He sighed as he fell onto his bed. He'd deal with one thing at a time. He laid his head on his pillow and didn't move.

The next day on the drive to school he decided to quiz Cassie about her mother and Mark. "Did you notice your mom and Mark? They looked as if they were making plans. Don't you think that is a good sign?" Cassie looked at Josh as if she was trying to read his mind.

"I did notice the two of them. I think my mom was happier than I've seen her in quite some time. I sincerely hope Mark can get her interested in the farm enough to help us keep her here."

She paused and then, "Josh, have you noticed we haven't had any episodes lately? Wonder why it has slowed down?"

Josh took the hint; change the subject. "I have noticed. Wonder if your mom has noticed?"

"I haven't discussed it with her lately. It's almost as if we are dancing around the hard topics." She stared out the window lost in her thoughts while Josh drove in silence also lost in his thoughts.

True to his word, Mark was back on Leigh's porch early the next morning. Leigh had to smile when she saw him in spite of her nervous dread. How was she going to tell him about her decision to move Cassie away from the house? She had to tell him; it wasn't fair for him to wait for a relationship that couldn't happen. Now was as good a time as any to lower the boom on her dearest sweetheart. She took a deep breath and opened the door to the most loving and kind eyes she had ever known.

She didn't have a chance to say anything. Mark swept her back into the house and in one movement engulfed Leigh in his embrace and kissed her deeply. Leigh found it easy…too easy, to return his kisses. Finally, Mark pulled away and announced that he had taken the day off from the supply store. He invited Leigh to a picnic up on the farm's pasture side. While pushing the guilt away, Leigh chose not to think of what had to happen and accepted his arm. Once they were on their way to the pasture she stopped. "Mark, don't we need some food and blankets?" She giggled.

Mark led her to his truck and pulled out a plastic bin filled with a picnic basket and blanket. She looked at him and gently touched his face. Their eyes locked again. She refused to allow the ugly truth find its way into their beautiful time together. They walked past the barns, past the fields that needed to be plowed and up into the hills.

The day had been a dream come true for the both of them. Leigh and Mark lay on the blanket looking at the autumn sky with contentment. They had laughed and loved and talked the entire day. It was as if they had never spent the last eighteen years apart. Yet, they had, and Leigh had a fifteen-year -old daughter to prove it.

Mark had been married once, but didn't have any kids. He was aware that Cassie was a significant part of his love's life, and he wanted more than anything to make her and her mother a part of his life. He had told Leigh how he felt and what he wanted. She had cried--his confession had touched her deeply. But she was also sad that Cassie and Mark might never have a chance to be any closer than what they were right now.

Mark reluctantly realized it was time to go back to the house as much as he wanted to stop time; it would not stand still. And most importantly, he didn't want Cassie to get angry with him for taking her mother before he had a chance to gain her trust. "Leigh, we need to get back. It is getting late, and the kids will be back from school in a couple of hours."

Leigh was surprised; they had been on that hillside all day long. It was the best day she had lived in a very long time. She shoved her joy to the back of her mind, making the day a memory to enjoy for many years to come. She took a deep rigid breath and set about tearing this incredible day apart and the man she would always love to pieces. "Mark, I must talk to you about something." Leigh's face had changed from a beautiful glow to a pale grey. "This is the hardest thing I have ever done." Mark felt the change in the atmosphere and sat up straight as a chill moved over his body.

"Leigh, please, you can tell me anything. I am here for you. I can tell you are concerned about something. I am not going to leave you alone, or allow you to leave me, ever again." These words brought the flood of tears once again. Leigh was beginning to wonder if she would ever be able to stop crying. Her heart was breaking. Mark felt confused. All he wanted to do was gather her up in his arms and protect her.

Leigh looked at Mark and decided she would tell him everything. "Don't interrupt me until I have finished. If you do, I swear I won't have the strength to finish." Mark shook his head in agreement and stared at Leigh intently. She closed her eyes. She dared not see his face as she broke the truth to him. Without looking at him or waiting for him to respond, she spilled the whole story. She told him about Cassie's discontent when they first moved here, and her change of heart once she met Josh. She told him about all the strange happenings in the house, and she told him of her decision to move back to Louisville in an attempt to protect Cassie. When she finished, she took a deep breath and slowly looked into Mark's face expecting to see the same hurt in his face as she was feeling. But, she was shocked by what she saw. Mark was smiling, almost laughing at her. Was he crazy? She had just told him she was leaving, and they could not be together.

"Mark, why are you smiling about all of this?" She stared at him in disbelief. "How can you take this so calmly when I have just told you this love we have can't be?"

Mark became alert, "You realize we love each other, Leigh? I have always known; I just wasn't sure you could see it."

"Mark, that isn't our problem. We have always loved each other and we always will. We just can't be together like regular people that love each other." As she took a loud breath and prepared to rant some more, Mark grabbed her and kissed her long and hard. When he allowed her to get some air, her mind had totally left her. As she tried to come back to earth, Mark pulled her to him again, but this time he kissed her lightly.

"I will never leave you, Leigh. You and I are meant to be together and face it; we are our own worst enemies." He turned her head to look into her eyes. "We will face this together and all the other turmoil that will follow. We will be together, and that is the only important fact, my love."

Leigh trying to gain her senses formed the word, "How?" But before her voice found sound, Mark had collected the food and the blanket and grabbed her hand. "We have to get back before I lose ground with your daughter. I have to get her to feel comfortable with me." Leigh followed without speaking. They were both silent in their own worlds, Leigh's face, full of confusion, and Mark's, full of joy.

When they got back to the house, the phone was ringing. Leigh answered, and Mark heard, "Anita, of course we will be there. Thank you for thinking of us." Mark allowed her some privacy with her call as he pulled out the contracts. He had to get these signed so the farmers could get the ground ready for the winter.

When Leigh came into the dining room, Mark had the papers on the table ready for her signature. She began shaking her head. Mark forced the pen in her hand. "Sign and if it doesn't work out for you here, I'll take care of the farmers next season, deal?" He pushed the pen firmly in her hand.

She relented and began signing. Mark smiled. First step to gaining his true love had just happened. Josh and Cassie came bursting into the dining room and greeted the two of them. "Hey you two. Looks as if you had a good day." Leigh quizzed.

"We did have a good day, Mom. Josh and I are grabbing a snack and going to the barn." Cassie and Josh grabbed some of the leftover sandwiches Leigh had laid on the table. They both took bites and floated out of the house. Leigh smiled. Mark moved close and caressed her shoulder.

She turned and looked wishfully at him. Mark squeezed tighter, "Be happy, this is going to be okay." He looked out the window and hesitated then announced he had to go; he was having dinner with Anita and Kyle next door.

Leigh snapped her head around to face him. "What? You are having dinner with Anita and Kyle?"

Mark slowly moved his head signaling "Yes."

Leigh smiled, "Anita." She moved closer to Mark, "Guess who else is going to be guests at Anita and Kyle's this evening."

Mark looked at her and slowly allowed the smile to form on his face. "Cassie and you are going to eat dinner at the Johnson's?" He began laughing. Leigh stared while he laughed, and finally joined him with the best laugh of the day.

Leigh decided to put it all out on the table. When Cassie and Josh came back to the house to announce they were going to Josh's barns, Leigh told them of the invitation for Cassie and her. She also said that Mark had been invited to dinner at the Johnson's. Cassie seemed okay with it and Leigh felt encouraged to push a little more.

"Since we are all here, and we are all going to the same place, why don't we all go over together? Would you two mind hauling two more guests over to the farm?"

Josh thought he'd better respond before Cassie saw what the world could already see—that Leigh and Mark were an item. "We'd love to chauffeur the two of you." He smiled down at Cassie, hoping for her approval. She didn't disappoint him.

"Sure, we can all fit in the truck. It's large, and we're going such a short distance. Come on let's go."

Mark and Leigh followed the two out to Josh's truck and squeezed into the cab. They laughed and talked easily on their ride to the Johnson farm. Leigh rang the doorbell, and the two posed outside the door for Anita's benefit. When Anita opened the door, her mouth flew open. She looked from one to the other and screamed, "Kyle. Come see what, or should I say who, is at our door."

She hugged them both and Kyle escorted them into the living room where they laughed and talked. It was as if they were back in high school. Cassie and Josh watched the four adults. They seemed so at ease with one another, so happy.

Josh thought this might be a good time to plant a seed. "As happy as they are, makes you wonder how your mom can even think of leaving. They all seem happier when they're together. Don't you think?"

Cassie watched her mother laugh and genuinely have fun with her friends. She was so different here than she was even before her dad had left. She couldn't allow her mother to lose this in her life. She snuggled in Josh's arms and closed her eyes. She had a feeling the possibility of them staying in Salyersville was becoming stronger.

Nineteen

After Cassie left for school the next day, Leigh found herself drinking her coffee in a state of bliss. Yesterday was a perfect day. She watched Cassie while they were all at Anita's, and she didn't see anything from her daughter that would indicate that she was upset with Leigh's closeness with Mark. She remembered the first day Cassie and she had gone to Caudill Feed and Supply. Cassie had been cold to Mark that day.

But now, Cassie was happier than she could ever remember. Leigh didn't want that joy to end. She had been through enough with the divorce and her father's remarriage. The move had taken its toll on them both, especially since the house had turned out to be haunted.

Leigh was still in a fog, reminiscing about all she and Mark had said and done yesterday, when the phone rang. She floated into the living room and answered. It was Anita. She quickly held the phone away from her ear. Anita was obviously excited about something. Leigh could hear Anita's voice clearly even when she had it held far away from her ear. "Leigh, I have it. I have been thinking about the house, and I have a theory. Are you ready?"

Leigh murmured, "Yes." She didn't know if she was or not, but with Anita the best answer is "yes." Because if Anita thought she wasn't ready to deal with a situation she would take the job of getting her ready.

"How long has it been since something has happened in the house? Think, Leigh. When was the last time?"

Leigh had already been thinking about this, "It was back when we first discussed leaving the house. Do you think whatever it is expects us to leave, so it is giving us a break?" Leigh nearly laughed.

Anita squealed, "No. You have stopped disturbing it."

Leigh looked at the phone and shouted in the phone herself, "ARE YOU CRAZY?"

Anita declared, "Absolutely not. Think about this. What if the spirit or ghost ... whatever it is was disturbed with the changes you were making to the house?"

Anita waited for a response from Leigh, but only silence met her. "What if your redecorating the house has caused the activity?"

Anita's theory wasn't new to Leigh. She had noticed the same thing Anita was pointing out to her. She had wondered more than once if her decorating had caused the lady of the house to show her discontent. Once she stopped decorating, the house had remained still. But, how could they prove that the house was upset because of all the decorating?

Leigh started to argue with Anita but then her mind kept flashing to the incidents and she realized it was time to acknowledge what was happening in her grandparent's house.

She had to admit that the incidents that happened to Cassie happened when they first came to live in the house. Could they have disturbed long lost spirits? Leigh looked around the house with a different perception than she had ever had of the home her grandparents had lovingly given her.

Finally, Leigh found her voice. "It is a sound theory, Anita, but how can we prove it?"

Anita's voice blared out of the phone even louder than usual, if possible. "That is what I am so excited about. What if we finished the kitchen and any other things we can find to refurbish, and see if we get any action?" Leigh looked at the phone as if it was Anita standing in front of her. "Have you completely lost it, Anita?"

Anita dismissed Leigh's question, "Listen, if we test this, we can find out not only how this is happening, but also we could have a good idea on how to stop it. The two of us will work on the house, and our goal will be to make the 'whatever' show itself and of course to finish the refurbishing of the kitchen."

As she waited for a response, she heard the defeat in Leigh's voice, "What if this plan doesn't work? Do I just start over? Tell me again, why do we want it to show itself?"

Anita didn't detour, "If it shows itself while we are working on the house, we will know why it's appearing and we can then work on taking care of the problem." She hesitated in wait of Leigh's excitement. When she didn't hear anything on the other end of the phone call, she plowed on, "Leigh, your Granddad and Grandma lived in that house their whole lives. Do you really think they would have left it for you to live in if they thought it was a danger to you or to Cassie?"

Finally, Leigh gained her thoughts enough to respond, "Okay, I get it Anita. Let's try it."

Anita hung up the phone, and before Leigh could drink her morning coffee, her friend was pounding on her door. Leigh was laughing before she even opened the door. "Are you sure you want to try this, Anita?"

Anita hugged her friend, "I am not losing my best friend again, ghost or no ghost."

They sat at the dining table drinking another cup of coffee while they planned what they would do today. Luckily, Leigh had not returned the supplies for the kitchen. Anita was so excited she couldn't contain her enthusiasm. Once finished with the last cup of coffee they made their way into the kitchen and began the chore of unpacking the paint and tile.

They worked all morning to finish painting the kitchen. Next, they started tiling behind the kitchen sink. Anita was losing her excitement since they had worked all morning without incident. She knew her friend, and she knew that Leigh had indeed experienced happenings. She hoped this worked; Leigh needed that extra nudge to persuade her that her life was here with her family.

Leigh could see the disappointment on Anita's face. "Let's have a snack and a rest okay?"

Anita agreed, and they made themselves tuna sandwiches and large glasses of ice tea. While they sat in the dining room Anita invited Leigh and Cassie to have Thanksgiving dinner with her family. Leigh gratefully accepted with the stipulation that Uncle Ray and Aunt Betty weren't upset about their invitation.

They sat for a while resting, talking about everything and anything except the one subject that hung heavy in the room; the reason for the day's work. Anita finally couldn't pretend it didn't exist, "Well, on the upside if we don't get any action today, the kitchen is going to look fabulous." Leigh choked on her drink of ice tea, laughing.

Anita looked bewildered, not sure why Leigh was laughing; she had been serious. Then she began laughing too, and by the time they finished, both were weak. Anita jumped from her seat, renewed and ready to try again. Leigh was not as eager as Anita to challenge the house. They worked at finishing the tiling and pulled the cabinet doors off their hinges for sanding and then painting. Leigh was amazed at the transformation of the kitchen. She had had high hopes for this house and for their lives in the house. But how could they stay? She felt her spirit lowering as they worked into the late afternoon. They had worked all day, and nothing had happened. They heard Josh's truck pull up and then the laughter of their two kids as they came into the house. "Hey, anybody home?" Cassie and Josh automatically found their way into the kitchen looking for food.

What they found were two tired moms and a kitchen that looked great. Cassie was shocked. She knew her mother had put away the supplies for the kitchen, yet here it was almost finished. She began to smile. "Mom, does this mean you have changed your mind?" She didn't wait for an answer. She ran to her mother and flung her arms around her neck. Leigh hugged her back and then looked in Cassie's face and without a word; Cassie understood there hadn't been any change in her mother's decision. She dropped her hands and hurt flooded her face. She didn't say another word to the women. "Josh, let's get some chips and go to the barn, okay?"

Josh looked at his mother, and then at Leigh. His brow

furrowed. Abruptly, he turned and followed Cassie out of the house. Leigh and Anita stood motionless until they heard Cassie's frantic shout for them to come to the barn.

Anita was scared that something had happened to Josh and didn't wait for Leigh. She raced to the barn to find Josh standing in front of a pile of tools stacked in a huge mound in the middle of the barn. Leigh came running in behind Anita. The farm tools were piled in the center of the barn. She felt the shivers begin to form in the pit of her stomach. How were the kids taking this? She looked from the tools piled on top of each other to her daughter. Cassie and Josh both seemed to be fine. How could everyone be calm about this?

Cassie refused to show how frightened she was. She had to make her mother see that not even this would make her want to leave. She began picking up the tools and arranging them in the appropriate places. Josh began helping without a word.

Anita found her voice and shouted, "Yes. It worked, Leigh."

Leigh was still motionless but finally looked around at her ecstatic friend and asked, "What now, Anita?"

Anita refused to hear the frustration in Leigh's voice. "Now we know that our Casper is telling us she isn't happy about the renovation. We now decide if she can tell you how to decorate or not. I'm thinking you are so close to finishing that it's not even a decision you need to worry about making."

Leigh looked at her friend with a crease wrinkling her brow. "Are you for real? How can this be a good thing? Doesn't this scare you for our kids?"

Anita looked steadily at Leigh, "It won't hurt either of them to pick the tools up and put them back in their place. There was no HARM done here!"

Leigh turned from the barn and walked back toward the house. Anita looked at Josh and Cassie and winked. Cassie found it hard to be as happy as Anita, but Josh's mom did make them all see the upside of the situation.

Anita followed Leigh back to the house ready to

persuade her that this was a good thing that had occurred. Instead, she saw Leigh standing in the dining room motionless. Anita rushed to her friend's side and then saw what had left Leigh motionless. There in the middle of the doorway was piled all of the remaining supplies in a pyramid of sorts. Anita couldn't allow Leigh to know how eerie this scene was for her. She touched Leigh's arm, "This is precisely what we wanted to happen, right?"

Leigh backed away from the sight and turned toward the living room. Anita followed. She would have to admit it was a little unnerving to be a witness to this strange occurrence. It was easy to talk about it but actually to be a part of this strangeness was a different thing altogether.

Leigh searched the room as if looking for some sign of where she was and what she was doing. She came to a stop, and Anita visually saw the calm wash over her friend. She turned to face Anita with newfound calm and peace. "Okay, what do we do next? I don't want to lose this house or the family and friends we love."

Anita smiled, "Now that's my girl. Let's sit down and decide what is next."

Twenty

Just as the friends sat down on the couch to decide what their next step would be, someone was at the door. Anita was over joyed to see Mark's face when she answered the knock. She grabbed him by the arm and dragged him into the dining room to witness the pile of supplies stacked in the entry of the kitchen. "This is what we came home to after witnessing the barn … and wait until you see the barn."

Mark mumbled, "I just came from the barn. The kids called me after Leigh and you came back to the house. They thought I might be able to help. I refuse to allow whatever this is run Leigh away from here again. It can't win."

Anita straightened her back, "I think she is ready to fight. She wants to stay as much as we want her to stay. You have got to believe that Mark."

She searched his face and was satisfied with what she saw. Mark knew deep in his heart that Leigh loved him as much as he loved her. "I know she does, and I'm going to make sure that she stays." Mark smiled at Anita and turned to go find Leigh. Anita dropped her tired body into a dining table chair and breathed, "Thank Goodness someone has their head on straight."

She pushed her body off the chair and began pulling the items from the middle of the entry and placing them in their appropriate place. She gave Mark and Leigh some extra time and then went to find them. She stopped to call Kyle to tell him what had happened. In only Anita's fashion, she told him of the barn and the eerie happenings there and then coming to the house to find even more eeriness. She explained her plan to force the happenings and how it had worked.

She hesitated and then she whispered, "Kyle, I don't know what to do now that we have gotten this far in the plan. What do we do now?" She told him about Mark and how love oozed from the both of them. Kyle laughed at his romantic wife. Hearing his laugh made her imagine how she sounded to him, and this made her laugh at herself. She felt so close to her husband at that moment. "I love you my husband."

Kyle smiled and told his wife, "I love you too, baby."

"Okay, enough of this, we have work to do. Will you do my chores and then come on over here? I think the kids have gone over to do Josh's work and will probably be back shortly."

"I'll be over soon, and I'll discuss this situation with Bessie and Mabel to see if they can come up with a plan." They both laughed at the vision of the cows having a conversation with Kyle. "Goodbye, darling. I'll see you soon."

"Goodbye, I love you." Anita felt better after talking with her husband. They fit together so well. He was the opposite of her. She was bullheaded and ready to challenge everything. He was strong and stood in the background waiting so he could finish the job she had started.

She wondered how the kids were taking all of this. They didn't know the full story. Should she have discussed her plan with Josh before she barged ahead? Too late, she was in too deep to stop now. She hoped the events of the day hadn't caused Cassie and Josh to stress out. She would have to apologize to the two when they returned.

Anita thought she had been away enough time for Mark and Leigh to have some private time. She tried to make noise before moving into the living room. They were sitting on the couch holding hands. Tears were streaming down Leigh's face as she fixed her eyes on Mark.

Anita couldn't help but smile at the sight. How those two lost each other so long ago was still a mystery to her. Hopefully, the time had come for the two to find each other again.

As she entered the room, the couple looked her way. She was curious about what they had discussed and if any decisions were made about their next steps. They both shook their heads no, but Mark added, "I just know I refuse to lose her to whatever is happening to this house." Leigh held on to his hand as if it were her lifeline.

As if on cue, someone knocked on the door. Anita walked toward the door, "That's probably Kyle. He's going to help us figure out what we should do now." She was so happy to see her husband standing there. She reached up and gave him a huge hug and pulled him in the house.

Kyle greeted both Mark and Leigh without a hint of surprise at the closeness they were showing. He was like his wife; he felt they should have been together from the start. He hoped they could make a go of it this time around.

Kyle sat down in Granddad's old chair. "I spoke with the kids before I came over and they described the barn to me. Anita tells me that the same thing happened in the kitchen." Leigh and Anita both nodded but said nothing for a moment. Anita sat down on the opposite chair and provided all the details once again.

She finished with confessing that it had been her idea to force the house to show itself so they would have an idea of why the occurrences were happening. "I know this is hard, but now we know that it doesn't like Leigh changing the house. Every time she starts changing the house, the incidents begin to occur. When she decided she had to leave and stopped working on the house, nothing happened for days. When we worked all day on the kitchen, it happened again. Don't you guys think this is good to know?"

Kyle began to laugh. "Well, you did get some answers but now what does Leigh do about living in the house? He had put the elephant right out on the table. "I am assuming you want to stay in Salyersville and on the farm?" He directed his question to Leigh.

She looked around her and then at Mark. "Cassie and I want to live here very much. I want to live in the house my grandparents gave me, but I don't know how to do that and make sure my daughter is safe. I don't want to leave town again. This farm is my home and my future; I am just at a loss on how to make it happen."

Mark spoke up, "We will work this out. We'll make sure Cassie and you are safe and that you don't have to move. I am not sure how we will do that at the moment. But, there has to be a way to solve this problem." He rubbed his forehead trying to make his brain come up with a solution.

Kyle cleared his throat, "Tell me Leigh, has anything that has happened caused harm to Cassie or you?"

Leigh looked up from her hands, "No, no one has been harmed." She hesitated before offering, "Except, Cassie has felt something breathe on her neck, and she felt a heaviness on her chest while lying on the couch one day."

Kyle continued, "Do you know if your grandparents ever had any problems with this type of thing or were they hurt in any way?"

Before Leigh could answer Kyle's question, Cassie and Josh came in the door. Josh volunteered, "We talked to Mammy about the house the other day. She said that Lizzy had told her about hearing loud sounds but that nothing ever hurt them and that the Howards learned to live with the house's weirdness without any problems." Cassie nodded her head in agreement.

Cassie directed her question to her mother. "Mammy said that a lady was killed by her husband in this house. Her name was Margret Ann Howard. Have you ever heard of this woman, Mom?"

Leigh became alert. "Margret Ann Howard? No, I have never heard of this lady until now." She shook her head in disbelief. "Her last name was Howard?" Leigh asked more to herself than to the others in the room, "Wonder if there is a connection to our family."

Josh offered, "Mammy didn't know if the lady was a relative of your granddad or not. She said that she had come from another county to marry the Cooper man."

Anita looked at her son, amazed at his maturity. She was so proud of him and glad that he was happier than she had seen him for a long time. She had to remind herself to have a talk with that boy about his trouble with Kari. Cassie had to know, and the time had come for Josh to show his loyalty to this girl. Obviously, he cared deeply about her.

Anita stole a peek at Cassie. She looked concerned for her mother or was her concern due to what or whom her mother was clinging to for dear life. Oh no, this was not the way Cassie needed to find out about her mother's long lost love. Anita moved behind Cassie and began waving at Mark profusely until she caught his attention. Immediately, Mark realized what Anita was trying to warn him about, and he dropped Leigh's hand and stood leaving Leigh dumbfounded. Mark walked over to Kyle and began discussing what needed to be done tonight. Anita watched the knowledge of the situation flow over Leigh's face, and she smiled. Anita could see she was upset but still had her wits about her. This was good.

She took another look at Cassie and saw Josh had come to the rescue. She wondered if Josh was helping out because he understood what was happening, or just because he couldn't help wanting to keep Cassie's attention averted to him. Her baby was in love and thank goodness; Cassie was just as emotional about him. She looked back at Leigh and took Mark's place beside her best friend. Leigh leaned into Anita's hearing range and thanked her for being the levelheaded one and for bringing her wonderful husband in to help. They both looked at Kyle and smiled but for different reasons.

After a while of hand holding, Anita decided everyone needed some refreshment, and she couldn't get her son off her mind. "Josh, could you help me in the kitchen for a second?"

Josh followed his mom into the kitchen and began pouring ice into glasses while Anita made some fresh tea. Anita paused, "Josh, when are you going to tell Cassie about Kari?"

Josh stopped, "What, why would I do that to her now?" He stared at his mother. He couldn't believe his mom wanted to discuss this NOW!

Anita dismissed his look and went on, "She needs to know and the longer you wait, the longer you risk losing her. She wants to know. She knows the worst of it, now tell her why." Anita didn't wait for a response from her son; she took the tray with ice tea and went to the living room.

Josh knew she was right, but this did not seem to be the best time. Then it dawned on him. It might be what Cassie needed to take her mind off of the bizarre happenings this evening. He asked Cassie to help him find some of the cookies they had raided this afternoon. Cassie came into the kitchen and gave him a quick hug and peck on the lips. "I'm so glad you are here, Josh."

"I wouldn't be anywhere else, Cassie. I want to share everything with you; the good and the bad." Josh thought about his mother's suggestion. She was right. It was time to tell Cassie the truth about Kari. He'd been asked to keep quiet about the situation for Kari's consideration but the time had come to tell Cassie everything.

He pulled her away from him and decided to go for it. "Cassie, I know this is going to seem like an awkward time for me to tell you about the whole Kari ordeal, but I want you to know the truth … if you still want to know." He studied her face. She was puzzled, anxious, nervous, confused, but determined to find out the truth.

"Please, I want to know. I have been waiting as patiently as possible." She braced herself for the worst.

Josh mustered up all the courage he could gather before beginning to explain. Once he began, the story fell out of his mouth. He wanted Cassie to know everything.

"Kari and I dated for a long time, over a year. We liked each other, but she was always demanding and never happy. I finally realized I needed to move away from the relationship and, so I broke up with her. Breaking up with her was hard, she was part of our group, and when we split she became more rude and meaner than ever. I was sad and wished my friends didn't have to suffer through my problem. Then one night I got a phone call."

He stopped and searched Cassie's face for her love and understanding. She was trying to follow along. So far, she hadn't heard anything that he couldn't have told her from the beginning. He began again. "Kari was in a bad way. Her voice was so slurred that I could hardly understand what she was saying. I finally got enough of the conversation to know that she was in trouble. She had taken several pills and was scared that she had killed herself. My mom and I rushed over to her house and made her dad take us into her room. She was lying in bed, looking like she was only sleeping. When her mother tried to wake her, she wouldn't wake up. She was lucky they were able to pump her stomach. She told me I was her only true friend. She told me she felt that she had nothing to live for if I wasn't in her life, if only as a friend. So, I began calling her every night partly because I wanted to make sure she didn't do anything stupid and because I wanted her to feel that someone was there for her." Once he finished he pulled his eyes from the floor to search her face again.

Cassie had tears running down her face. He moved close to her, "Cassie, I am truly sorry. Please don't cry. I swear to you; I have never in my life felt about another girl the way I feel about you. " He wiped the tears from her face as he whispered, "and I'll never feel for another girl the way I feel about you." He awkwardly wiped the tears from his face. "Please forgive me."

She looked through her tears finding his eyes as she caressed the side of his face. "Forgive you for what? You are the kindest and most loving person, and you're mine." She reached up to place a quick kiss on his lips. "Thank you so much for telling me." She pulled her hand behind his neck and pulled him to her lips. He obliged eagerly.

They held each other for as long as possible without drawing suspicion and decided they had better join the adults. As they walked toward the living room, Cassie stopped and turned to Josh, "Have you noticed the way Mark and Mom are looking at each other? When did that happen? Have I been so clueless that I didn't even see a romance developing?"

Josh started laughing so hard Cassie thought for a moment that the lady of the house had tickled him. "What is so funny?"

He tried to stop long enough to let Cassie in on the history between her mom and Mark. But first he had to make sure she was okay. "Are you okay with the two of them liking each other?" He examined her face for evidence that words wouldn't give him. He found a happy and perfectly 'okay' Cassie. He smiled, not even the house could bring his mood down tonight. "Have a seat, I have a lot to tell you, little girl."

Once Cassie knew the whole story she was genuinely happy her mom was going to have happiness in her life again. She realized that her mother was sacrificing her happiness for her. She felt guilty for treating her mother as if she were trying to ruin her life. She understood that Leigh was only trying to protect her. She ran into the living room and straight to her mother. She hugged her mom with all her strength. Leigh hugged her daughter back. Cassie's eyes danced as she told her mother what she had discovered and how happy she was for her.

Mark had been staying in the background behind Kyle almost afraid to show himself. He couldn't bare losing Leigh, and this young girl was the one thing that he could not compete with nor did he want to put himself between mother and daughter. Kyle reached behind his back and slapped Mark on the back, "Congratulations. Looks like you have Cassie's blessing."

Mark moved in front of Kyle and found Cassie's eyes. He didn't say a word, but Cassie knew what he was asking. She appreciated his delicate handling of the situation. She just nodded her acceptance and smiled at him. He smiled back. He felt like he would faint but held on, not wanting to miss anything about this incredible night.

Anita was hugging Josh so tight he was squirming. Her tears were flowing. Josh was so pleased that he had revealed the stupid secret that had almost cost him this wonderful girl, and he felt relieved that it was over. Cassie was fine with his reason for calling Kari and more than that; she was okay that Mark and her mom had become an item. And, he had the best parents in the world. He squeezed his mom back as hard as she was squeezing him.

Finally, Kyle, the sensible one, got everyone back to the issue at hand. "Okay, we have to decide what we want to do about the house. I have a suggestion. We can't leave Leigh and Cassie alone in the house for a while since we are not one-hundred percent sure of what will occur. So, why don't the girls go to our house for the night and the boys will stay in this house? Just until we're sure that whatever is in the house isn't going to harm anyone."

Anita hugged her husband. "I knew my man would come up with a solution. I love the thought of a slumber party. What do you say girls? Are you up for a night of girl talk?"

Leigh hesitated, "I don't want to leave my home. And, I don't want to put you guys out. You have been so good to Cassie and me already."

Anita shrieked, "We're family. Why would you think it would be any different? Now, come on, let's leave these brave, strong, handsome men alone to protect us, shall we?"

Leigh and Cassie grabbed their pajamas and told the men they would be back in the morning. They kissed their men and left them to face the lady of the house.

Anita was full of energy and joy and she was contagious. They had a great time driving back to Anita and Kyle's farm. Cassie took Josh's bed and Leigh slept in the guest room. They all had a somber moment when they thought about the men sleeping in the house. It didn't last long; Anita made sure of that. She was constantly laughing and causing Leigh and Cassie to laugh. She made her way to her bedroom and bid a goodnight to the two ladies before retiring to her room.

Cassie lay in Josh's bed looking around the room. Her boyfriend's room. She felt closer to him while she was in his personal space. She didn't know if it was her imagination, but she'd swear she could smell him.

She pulled his pillow to her face and inhaled the scents Josh had left. His room was very much like she had imagined, the basic bed and chest, a desk that rested under the window. From the bed, Cassie could look out the window and see most of the barns across the yard. She smiled. Josh would want to be able to see the activities that happened at the hub of the farm. He was a farmer through and through. She lay in his bed and replayed the afternoon's events. Wow. Life had come flooding down on her quickly. She smiled when she realized that her problem of moving was likely solved. Thank you, Mark.

For the first time in a very long time, Cassie snuggled under the covers without thinking about falling asleep—she was sleeping.

The next morning Leigh stumbled out of her room to find Anita making coffee. She was surprised. She felt certain she would be first to rise. Both women were eager to find out how the men had fared in her house. Before Anita filled their mugs with steaming coffee, Cassie popped out of Josh's room. Leigh marveled at how alert and happy Cassie looked. Seeing her daughter so happy made Leigh more determined to beat this thing with her house. She turned to Anita, "Ready to break up the party down the road?" She hoped her voice didn't give her fears and stress away.

Anita smiled and nodded. "Come on girls, we'll probably have to wake those lazy men. They all laughed at the picture this created in their minds and filed out the door. Anita drove the Ward ladies back to their house so they could get ready for the day and Kyle told her that the house was quiet and calm. Anita frowned, "I hope that doesn't mean it is waiting for Leigh and Cassie."

Realizing she had voiced this concern out loud she tried to cover by dismissing it with a wave of her hand. "Oh well, there have been many days and nights that Leigh and Cassie haven't experienced anything weird. But, we should keep a check on the house for a while, don't you think?" She turned to Kyle for an answer.

Kyle and Mark agreed to the same arrangement as the night before, at least for the next few days. Anita being the planner that she was, created a routine for the girls to go to Anita's at night while Kyle, Josh, and Mark stayed in

Leigh's house. The Howard house remained peaceful with no incidents while the men slept there.

After two weeks, the group determined that the house was fine and that there was no harm for Leigh and Cassie. Mark and Josh stayed close during the evening hours only going home at bedtime. Cassie finally got the nerve to ask Leigh about the move. Leigh looked at her daughter. "If everything stays as safe as it is right now, I will agree to keep you here. That is all I can give you. I will not put your life in danger."

Cassie couldn't wait to tell Josh the good news. She called Jessica and Megan and told them she was sorry, but her plans had changed. She was going to stay at her new home. She told them she missed them, but she had found some really great friends in Salyersville. She put her phone away and scooted closer to Josh as he drove toward school.

Leigh felt relieved after she officially told all of her loved ones of her decision to stay in the house. She called Mark, "Well, I told Cassie we would stay in the house as long as there didn't seem to be any harmful energy."

Mark quickly took the lead, "Let's celebrate. Get ready; I'm coming to take you on another picnic. Let's take some time to enjoy each other."

Leigh smiled, "I'd love to go on a picnic with you, Mark." She hung up the phone and busied herself getting ready for her date. She came out of her bedroom dressed for a picnic and saw Anita walking through the dining room into the kitchen.

She called. "Anita, how did you get in here? I could have sworn I locked the door when Cassie left for school."

That was funny; she went on into the kitchen without answering her. She was probably getting coffee ready for the two of them. She went in to help her with the coffee but no one was in the kitchen. She stopped in her tracks and then smiled.

She wasn't giving up her home to this strange entity … but she could be persuaded to share it.

"Okay, lady," she said in an audible voice, "Let's make this our home, shall we? I'll share if you will." Leigh didn't wait for an answer. She picked up the coffeepot and turned to pour her coffee in her favorite coffee mug. She stopped midway through her turn.

On Grandma Lizzy's table was her favorite coffee mug placed in prominent view. Alongside it was a spoon for her sugar. The spoon was perfectly centered on a cloth napkin. Leigh had never seen the white linen napkin until that morning. Was it one of Grandma Lizzy's? She moved closer to the table. The napkin was old but made of fine linen. It was as white and crisp as a new day.

She noticed something on one corner of the napkin. Someone had embroidered the initials "MAC". Leigh tried to remember those initials. They seemed familiar somehow. OMG—"MAC" was for Margret Ann Cooper, the beautiful young woman who had lived in the house long ago. This was the woman Mammy had told Cassie and Josh about.

Leigh smiled as she filled her mug with fresh coffee. Using the carefully placed spoon, she added sugar and stirred the white granules; dissolving into sweet flavor. Her first cup of the day; and a beautiful day it would be.

 **Vivian Ward Crump** is a short story author, first time novelist, and a teacher of writing.

Vivian's passion for writing has always influenced her chosen career as a language arts teacher. Vivian's middle school students were motivators in her decision to publish her novel, Lingering Soul of The House, a young adult novel, dealing with the paranormal, romance, and the problems that teenagers face in today's world.

The novel takes place in her hometown of Salyersville, Kentucky, located at the foothills of the Appalachian Mountains. Vivian grew up on a farm similar to the one she describes in Lingering Soul of the House.

The paranormal events in the story are based on real family legend as told by her grandmother about the house she lived in most of her life. The house is still owned by the family and is occupied by relatives in Eastern Kentucky.

Lingering Soul of the House is the first book in the Mountain Hauntings trilogy. The second book will be released in 2015 and the third is scheduled for release in 2016.

Turn the page for a sneak peak at Stranger Neighbor, the second book in the Mountain Hauntings Trilogy.

A haunting and romantic companion to The Lingering Soul of the House.

Stranger Neighbor

One

Life as she had always known was quickly dwindling away. Sarah made her way down the walkway, anxious to see her boyfriend who was sitting in his old blue Chevy pickup, waiting for her. This was the same routine they had followed ever since Jake had turned sixteen and got his driver's license. Every day was the same; Jake pulled his truck up to her house and waited. He never rushed her although she knew that there were times when he was aggravated with her for taking so long to come out of her house. On these occasions, he'd sit looking out the window as if he was examining the farm for the first time and had no time to look at Sarah. She always greeted him with a cheerful 'good morning.' hoping to catch his gaze. He answered but always without looking at her, choosing instead to examine the land that he saw every day. Sarah had learned to give him this moment and sit quietly until they had pulled out of the drive and were on their way to school. That was about the length of time it took Jake to get in a good mood and pull her up next to him in the truck.

She understood Jake's annoyance. Most mornings she rushed out giving them just enough time to make it to their first period class before being counted tardy. Since they lived about ten miles out of town, the trip took about twenty minutes (if Jake was in a rush). Sarah didn't like it when they had to rush. She considered this time their time away from everything going on around them. They used this time to enjoy one another and the drive. It was her favorite time of the day.

Today, enjoying each other, while ignoring everything that was going on around them, would be hard. The thing that bothered Sarah the most was sitting next to her— Jake. He was leaving…and as much as she wanted to put it out of her mind so they could enjoy their last days, seeing his cute face brought a stabbing reminder of his impending absence.

Sarah was determined to make these last days as pleasant as possible. She refused to think of the upcoming time when she and Jake wouldn't be with each other every day. They had always been close even when they were young. Jake lived down the road from her, about three miles away from her family's farm. They had grown up as best friends. Although Jake was nearly a year older, they were in the same grade in school. Their parents had been putting the two of them together even before they knew they wanted to be together.

This morning she walked briskly to his pick-up, not

wanting to miss a moment with him. She felt if she spent enough time with him she could bank up their time and use it throughout the summer while he was away. Realistically she knew this wasn't true. She would miss her boyfriend tremendously when he was gone. They had discussed his leaving when he had received his acceptance to the Young Male Appalachian Academic Achievement Program from the University of Kentucky. They both had planned for the upcoming separation all winter and spring. Sarah was bracing herself for her lonely summer while Jake got more excited every day for his good fortune--studying with the Medical College at the University of Kentucky.

As summer came closer, thinking about her loneliness was almost more than Sarah could bear. Summer was her favorite time of the year, but this summer was going to be miserable. She couldn't even count on Cassie, her best friend, to help see her through the sadness. Cassie had announced last week that she would be going back to Louisville to visit her dad for a month during summer vacation. Sarah had been happy for Cassie but felt very sorry for her imminent loneliness. What would she do alone in Salyersville, ALL SUMMER LONG?

Reaching the truck she bounced up into the passenger's seat and leaned over to get her good-morning kiss. Jake did not disappoint her. Their morning kiss was beginning to linger longer and longer as their time together grew shorter. She would have stayed with her lips tangled with Jake's for the entire day had he not pulled her away. He chuckled. "Gosh, girl, you are in a loving mood this morning, not that I'm complaining." He flashed his smile at her as he caressed her hair. She returned his smile, but it was half-hearted. Sarah moved closer to his ear and whispered. "Good Morning."

Jake turned away, concentrating on putting the truck in

gear and pulling onto the main road that would take them to Salyersville and to school.

He had not said anything about her sad face although he had noticed. He was sure that once summer was here, and Sarah was in a routine she would be okay. He hated that he would not be allowed to call her for two whole months. The YMAA strictly forbid students from calling home. He would only be allowed one Sunday evening for visitors, and that wouldn't happen until midway through the program. He didn't mind at all except for Sarah. He would miss her so much, but this was an opportunity he could not pass up. This summer was the beginning of his journey to becoming a doctor, and someday, when this summer was just a memory, he and Sarah would smile again.

Jake had asked his mom to make sure Sarah was okay during the summer. She promised to keep Sarah busy while he was away. She reminded him of all the events that happen during Buffalo Creek summers. Their community worked hard so when they got a chance; everyone joined in on the fun. The one event that was always everyone's favorite was having a picnic on the farm of a neighbor who volunteered their pasture as the location of the daylong event.

This year Jake's parents had offered up their east pasture since they had moved all the livestock to the woods behind the barn. Jake had felt a touch of sadness when his mom had told him about their decision to host the picnic this year. He knew that all the planning and preparing would be finished before he returned home. At least he would get home in time to enjoy the picnic. His mom said it would be his "coming home" party.

This morning, both of them were deep in thought about the upcoming summer. He could see that Sarah was trying very hard to hide her emotions. She sat looking out the window with a smile pasted on her lips. He had known this girl his whole life, and he knew she was hiding behind this smile. He guessed he also was hiding with his upbeat chatter and jokes. It was hard to face the fact that the two of them would not be seeing each other for so long.

He told his mom how much he would miss Sarah while he was gone. "It will be good for both of you." She had told him. "This summer will be a test of how devoted you are to each other. If the two of you make it through the summer, and the different experiences each of you will have, and you still feel the same closeness, you will know that what you have is real." She had gone on to say, "Jake, if it isn't there after the separation--better to know now than down the road."

He understood what his mom was saying … their whole lives were spent joined as a couple. He knew in his heart that his love for Sarah was a love that only happens once. He was sure that she felt the same. The families wanted the best for the two of them, and if it worked out, they would be ecstatic.

Their families were good friends. His father and Sarah's father were best friends and shared work on their farms, often helping each other out. Jake's dad, Morris, had moved to Buffalo Creek when he married Jake's mom, Alma. Alma's family had owned the Gamble farm for several generations. Jim, Sarah's dad, always kidded Morris about being a 'transplant.' Since Jim had always lived in the county of Magoffin, as a native, he felt he had bragging rights. Although, Sarah's mom often reminded her husband that he was a city boy from the great town of Salyersville. This fact brought giggles from anyone listening since Salyersville's population was only nine or ten thousand people, and that included the people living out in the county seat, like the Collin's and the Arnett's.

Just like Alma, Sarah's mom, Sandy, had lived on the farm her whole life except for the eight years she moved away to attend college. She had become the first veterinarian resident in the county of Magoffin. She was one of a few in the surrounding counties but the only female vet. In the foothills of this Appalachian community, this fact had made her career a struggle at first. Nowadays she was busier than she wanted, and her practice took her to neighboring counties as well as throughout Magoffin.

Alma was about four years younger than Sandy, so even though they had been neighbors during their childhood they had not been close until they both began raising their families. Now they were best friends, helping with work when each other's farms needed major attention.

Jake grabbed his girlfriend's hand as he stopped his pickup in front of Salyersville High. He pulled her to him for one last kiss before going to class. Sarah's smile became genuine when their lips parted, and she pushed him away and jumped out of the truck, racing to the driver's side. Jake locked the door by the time she made it to his side. He kissed her on top of her head as if she were a little sister. He dropped his arms, reached for her hand, and they ran to the entrance of the building racing to their separate classes.

Sarah could not wait until lunch. She wanted to meet up with Cassie and Josh along with their other friends. Their group was close, and she was hopeful that the gang staying in Salyersville over summer vacation would help keep her busy while Jake was at UK. As she walked into the cafeteria, she saw them in their usual spot. Cassie and Josh were sitting to one side of the table while Seth and Logan were fooling around telling jokes on each other making everyone laugh. Jake was sitting on the other end of the table with her seat waiting. She smiled and made her way to his side. She gave him a quick peck on the lips and smiled at Cassie. She was so glad her friend had moved to Magoffin from Louisville.

Cassie's mom had grown up on Lick Creek near Buffalo but married and moved to the western part of Kentucky. Cassie had moved back to her great-grandparents' home because of her parents' divorce. At first Cassie had issues about the move; blaming her mother for having to leave her home. Yet, when faced with leaving because of weird things happening in her grandparents' house, Cassie fought like crazy to stay in Magoffin. Sarah knew that Cassie wanted to stay in Magoffin mainly because of Josh, but she also knew she considered Sarah her best friend. Sarah had never had a best friend except for Jake; so having a girl best friend had been awesome for the last year. This thought brought a fleeting sadness because Cassie would be leaving her this summer too. She brightened when she remembered that Cassie and she could keep in touch, and she would come home in a month.

"Hey, guys. How's everybody today?" She dropped her books on the table and looked over at Cassie.

"Hey, Sarah, how are you? It has been a long morning for me. I am so ready for this school year to be over," Cassie pouted.

Sarah nodded agreement although she did not feel the same way. She knew that her summer would mean long, lonely days of working on the farm with only old people to keep her company. What a bummer. She remembered her promise to Cassie that she would help her mom out on their farm while Cassie was away. "Cassie, did you ask your mom what she wanted me to do while you are away?"

Cassie smiled at her friend, "I did talk with her about it. Sarah, Mom, is so happy you'll be visiting and helping with the farm chores. I can't thank you enough."

"I am more than happy to help out. Did she have a list of chores for me yet?"

"No, I think she is just happy someone will be there to keep her company while I'm in Louisville. You won't mind the house, will you? I would totally understand if you don't want to hang around with the stuff that sometimes happens." Cassie searched Sarah's face for an answer.

It was only last year that Cassie had almost moved from her great-grandparents' home because of unexplained occurrences that happened in the house and on the farm. Cassie's mother was scared for her and wanted to move back to Louisville, but fortunately the house had settled down so that the Wards felt safe to stay. Later Cassie had revealed to Sarah that things still occurred in the house but not near as severe as when her mother and she first moved into the place.

Sarah did not care that Cassie's house was full of paranormal incidents. She had been at the Howard Farm plenty of times and had never seen anything. Only Josh's family, Sarah, and Cassie's mom's friend Mark knew about the happenings at the Ward's home. Sarah reassured her friend she did not mind going to her home and would find visiting her mom as helpful for her loneliness as Cassie's mom.

As they ate their lunch, everyone was talking about their summer plans—except Sarah. She sat quietly and listened to the excitement around the table. Jake was aware of his girlfriend's mood and found her hand with his, giving it a squeeze and releasing only slightly, keeping her securely close to him. She squeezed back, and her blue eyes brightened.

At the end of the lunch period, they all rose to face the next part of the day. Since Sarah had Biology and Jake had Chemistry they could walk over to the Science building together. They made it to the entrance and Sarah went to her class on the first floor while Jake took the stairs to the third floor, finding his class. They wouldn't see each other again until it was time to go home.

That afternoon, Sarah made it back to the truck before Jake. She leaned against the truck, waiting while Jake finished his class. As she looked about her, students were lazily making their way out of the school and into the parking lot searching for their cars and buses. The atmosphere of the school was changing. Everyone, including the teachers, was winding down. The days of her junior year were numbered. Before long she and Jake would be seniors. Senior year! She had dreamed of this year her whole life.

She and Jake both wanted to attend the University of Kentucky. Jake wanted to become a doctor, and she wanted to follow her mother's footsteps and become a veterinarian. She just had to make it through these lonely weeks of summer and life would be back on track. Her friend Cassie had her mind set on attending the University of Louisville and so of course, Josh would follow her.

As Sarah daydreamed, her eyes caught a glimpse of someone she had never seen on campus. If she had seen this person she would have remembered. He was tall … at least as tall as Jake, who was six-four. He had beautiful black hair with eyes that made you look even at a distance. Who was he? He didn't look as if he belonged in Magoffin.

She watched him stroll over to a cherry red BMW sitting in the parking lot. Just as he opened the sleek door to the car, Jake came bouncing over. She forgot all about the boy in the cherry red BMW and turned to the light of her life. She giggled and tried to be sexy as she murmured. "Hey, handsome. Can a girl get a lift?"

Jake laughed, "That might be arranged." He sauntered over to the door of the passenger side of his truck and with a grand gesture bowed and motioned for her to enter the truck.

Sarah giggled and with the same grandness made her way to the front seat of Jake's truck. "Thank you, kind sir." She reached for his face and gave him a peck on his right cheek. She could smell his distinct scent, and she logged it to her memory. She'd use it later when she needed to remember things about him to get her through the long days of loneliness.

The drive home was easier and lighter than the morning had been. They both took turns manipulating the conversation by discussing everything from the upcoming four-wheeler outing to Sarah's observation of the new kid on campus. Jake had not seen the owner of the new BMW, but he had definitely seen the BMW. He wondered how a kid could drive a car that expensive--especially in Eastern Kentucky. Sarah wondered too. She described the boy she saw walking to the car to Jake but chose not to mention how cute he was, and how his eyes pulled you in to him.

Just as Jake was asking if she knew his name, the red BMW raced past them. Jake and Sarah looked at each other with wide eyes. Jake mumbled, "What the...." He didn't need to finish; Sarah knew what he was thinking. What was going on? Just as Sarah had wrapped her brain around the scene of a BMW with a teenager at the wheel, they saw the red car in front of them--headed toward Buffalo Creek. Why on earth would this stranger be driving up their little out of the way road? What was he doing in their neighborhood? How had he found Buffalo Creek?

Neither spoke. They couldn't believe their eyes. What was this stranger doing in the foothills of the Appalachia?

VIVIAN WARD CRUMP

Stay Connected to Vivian

You will find Vivian living in Shelbyville, Kentucky with her family and her faithful dog, Shelby, who has decided it's her job to sit close by while Vivian works on her writing.

If you want to read more of **Stranger Neighbor** send an email to viviancrump@gmail.com and she will send you the next two chapters for free. You can like Vivian Ward Crump on Facebook and talk to her on Twitter @VivianWardCrum1.

If you enjoyed reading **Lingering Soul of the House**, you can leave a review on her wall or news feed.

Thank you.

ACKNOWLEDGMENTS

I have always taught my students to write about what they know so when I began writing this book I pulled from my own advice. I took my childhood home, added drama and make-believe to the mix, and Lingering Souls of the House was born.

So thank you Salyersville, Kentucky, for being a great place to grow up. Thank you Mamaw Mayzina, for your house with all the lingering souls that haunt this story. Thank you for all the tales you told us when I was a child.

Thank you Peggy DeKay and Kelci Risner-Burkel for reading and helping me mold this story. Your support and advice was invaluable.

And most of all, thank you to my family and friends that have supported my dream. You have cheered me on and given me support when I felt overwhelmed.